IF YOU HEAR HOOFBEATS

A JOSIE HARJO NOVEL

CATHERINE SEQUEIRA

IF YOU HEAR HOOFBEATS

Cover design by Gareth Clegg

Published by Barcelos Publishing, LLC, Sacramento, CA, USA

The Library of Congress Cataloging-in-Publication Data is available upon request.

ISBN 9798988723134 (trade paperback)

ISBN 9798988723141 (hardback)

ISBN 9798988723158 (ebook)

First Edition: February 2024

Printed in the United States of America

To all the veterinarians.
You got this.

CHAPTER
ONE

The dead steer smelled like shit, and we hadn't even cut into it yet. The carcass had probably been baking in the Oklahoma summer sun for a good two to three days before the rancher decided to mosey it on in. Now, the steer was lying on its side on the cool, metal necropsy table, its abdomen green-tinged and so bloated that the front and back legs practically pointed straight up in the air.

I sighed.

I knew the stench of this steer would stick to me like a fly on a turd. Even with coveralls, the fumes always seemed to find a way to linger on my hair and skin.

I had my first Match date tonight and didn't want to show up reeking like a dead animal.

In a meager attempt to reduce the surface area for the smell to penetrate, I wound my dark, wavy hair into a bun, using a pen to hold it all together.

The gloves went on with a *snap*, and I grabbed my necropsy knife. I flicked the tight skin over the steer's abdomen, and a light *thud* sounded.

Dustin let out a deep laugh. "Yee-haw! I love the smell of rotting flesh in the morning!" he said with a thick Oklahoma twang as he stepped back out of range, leaving me to decompression duty.

Sure, I outranked him and could have pushed him into the line of fire. But I wasn't that kind of person and was willing to take one for the team.

Dressed in short-sleeved coveralls and rubber boots, Dustin stood about six and a half feet tall. He was skinny but strong; he had to be when hauling large animal guts around all day. Being in his late forties, he was about ten or fifteen years older than me. His brown, graying hair was kept short, but he boasted a large bushy beard. I'd always wondered why he had facial hair; it tended to catch bits of rumen contents and flecks of blood when we were working.

Dustin was the lab's only full-time necropsy technician. He was here when I started this job, and we'd become pretty tight over the last six years. I'd taken this position straight from my residency, wide-eyed and bushy-tailed. He'd taught me more than any of the faculty ever had, and always in a friendly way. I was eternally grateful to have such a cool coworker; a necropsy tech could really make or break a gig.

I angled my body away from the steer, stepping back as far as I could. Holding my knife like a rapier, I stabbed through the abdominal skin. With some pressure, the knife popped through. A loud, shrill hissing sound echoed through the necropsy room as the abdomen started to deflate, and a putrid stench filled the air.

I took several steps back, trying to escape the noxious fumes.

Dustin grimaced. "Oh, dang. This one's real bad."

We'd both cut up our fair share of rotten animals. But, when he complained, I knew it was truly nasty. He'd been working on the necropsy floor for over twenty years. Time had a way of helping the brain tune out even the rankest of carcasses. The years of formalin exposure had also dampened his sense of smell. If the dead steer's odor had made it to what was left of his fried olfactory bulbs, then I was screwed.

"Why do they always wait so long to bring 'em in?" he asked rhetorically, shaking his head as the whistle of the escaping gas slowly petered out.

For whatever reason, some ranchers liked to wait a good day or two before hauling in a dead animal. I'd never figured out why. If you were worried about more animals dying, wouldn't you want to bring a dead one in as soon as possible? I guessed people were just busy. Regardless of the reason, Oklahoma summers were always rough on the necropsy floor.

"At least there are no maggots," I commented, grasping at straws.

"That we know of," he corrected, tossing me a mischievous smile.

I fought back a gag at the thought. As much as I was used to death, I loathed maggots. They made this crinkly sound like bubble wrap when they poured out of a dead animal and wriggled on the necropsy table.

"Not cool, man. Not cool." I shook my head, pretending to be hurt, and then flashed him a smile to let him know all was good.

I held up the front leg and stabbed into the axilla, looking across the wide table at him. "You gonna help me or what?" I teased.

"I don't know. I was just 'bout to take my afternoon break," he said as he moved over to assist.

It was an idle threat and all part of our usual friendly banter. Dustin was a good dude. He knew how to keep things light so the bad days didn't weigh too hard. The animal cruelty cases were the worst and were invariably followed by a day or two of depression. Dustin was always there to help bring me back up, reminding me how important our jobs were.

He grabbed the front leg, pulling it to the opposite side of the table as I extended my cut toward the neck and then back toward the flank.

"At least the skin isn't sloughing off," he said in all seriousness this time.

"Very true," I conceded.

I'd also had the not-pleasure of cutting up a few carcasses so far gone that the skin just wiped away when I touched it. Not only were those cases pretty much a wash, but when an animal this large got slippery, injuries could happen.

With the front leg reflected, we moved to the rear leg.

He held the back leg up as I made a stab in the inguinal region, making quick slices to cut the attachments. With the hip joint exposed, I cut the ligament, and Dustin pulled the leg back with a *pop*.

"Don't you have a date tonight, Doc?" Dustin asked, interrupting my thoughts.

"Yeeeah," I said in my best Lumbergh voice.

Dustin laughed. "You know this ain't gonna wash off, right?"

Another rhetorical question.

I glared at him, fighting back a smile.

I stepped back and wiped my arm across my forehead, knife still clasped in my right hand. It was hard work cutting up a steer, and I was already breaking a sweat.

Please don't add B.O. to the wonderful bouquet you've already got cooking, Josie.

"Why is your date on a Thursday anyway? That's kinda weird," Dustin said.

With the front and back legs reflected, I cut the skin away from the abdominal wall as I said, "I guess he's busy with work, and this was the only evening he had free."

Dustin looked doubtful.

Can't say I blamed him. I kinda felt the same way, but my Match date was cute, and it had been a barren stretch in the romance department.

With the skin reflected, I stepped back and let out a dejected sigh. The underlying abdominal wall was green-tinged. That particular shade of green was bad juju on the necropsy floor; it often meant everything inside would be liquified.

As if reading my thoughts, Dustin mused, "It's gonna be soup in there."

"Yep," I said, trying to roll with it. "Hope it isn't gastrointestinal disease."

The intestines, stuffed with a plethora of microflora when alive, turned into bacteria-baby factories after the normal checks and balances were trashed at death. The guts always autolyzed first, quickly turning to mush. It was those same baby-making factories that produced the gas that was probably going to ruin my date tonight.

I cut through the abdominal wall and pulled the muscle back. Sure enough, the intestines were like soup, and I knew they would dissolve in my hand as soon as I tried to take them out. I decided to see what the chest held before I tried to do anything with the abdominal organs.

After poking the diaphragm with the tip of my knife, a slight rush of air escaped as the diaphragm went flaccid. This was a hissing sound we *wanted* to hear. It meant there had been negative pressure in the chest, which was normal.

Following a well-practiced routine, I cut a C-shape in the diaphragm.

Knowing what would come next, Dustin was already there with the loppers and handed them to me. The guy was a master on the necropsy floor. He could open a large animal in about fifteen minutes and have all of the internal organs removed in less than that. He was also a magician with a bandsaw and could open a large animal's spinal column like it was butter. He always knew what I would need next.

I stabbed the knife into the meaty part of the steer's rear leg, a safe place to stash it when not in use. I grabbed the loppers, hooking the longer of the curved blades around the first rib. Crunching my way through the ribs toward the head, sweat began to drip down my temples. I passed the loppers back over to Dustin, who did the opposite side.

Grabbing my knife from its meat-sheath, I cut a makeshift handle in the intercostal muscles and pulled the rib cage back, slicing through the soft tissues until it finally came clear. I tossed the chest wall into the offal bin, where it landed with a loud *slurp*.

"Thank sweet baby Jesus," Dustin said once he'd had a look into the thoracic cavity.

Even though he wasn't a trained veterinary pathologist, he knew a good lesion when he saw one.

Through the rot, the cause of death was immediately obvious. Over fifty percent of the lung lobes were dark red and firm, with dozens of scattered, pinpoint white dots. It was a slam dunk bacterial pneumonia or "bovine respiratory disease complex" to those in the know.

I looked at him with one eyebrow raised. "We still have to look at everything, you know."

"Yeah, yeah." He waved me off. "But I won't tell anyone if you do a cursory once-over."

I smirked because, of course, Dustin was right. We'd collect lung samples for microbiology, hoping to culture something more than post-mortem bacteria. Another section of the lung would go off for viral testing. Though it didn't matter for this steer, the additional testing may help the other cattle in the herd. After that, it would just be a quick once-over of the other organs to make sure it wasn't a two-fer. Dustin could handle that. And thankfully, histology wasn't needed. The organs were too soupy to look at anything under the microscope anyway.

Just as we were finishing up, Gerald came out on the floor, a handkerchief held over his nose.

"Oy! Please put a lab coat and boots on, Dr. Richter," Dustin called out as he heaved the dissected abdominal organs into the offal bin.

Gerald rolled his eyes and returned a few minutes later wearing blue shoe covers and a lab coat, hankie still held tightly over his nose.

"Is this the BRD case?" Gerald asked, his normally shrill voice muffled by the hankie.

I nodded, dropping the dissected pluck into the offal bin. Covered in blood, I walked over to him.

"Will you be sending samples of the lung for culture? Obviously, that's indicated in a case like this." Gerald wagged his hand at the carcass.

"Yes, Dustin will bring them to the lab as soon as we're cleaned up," I said, unable to hide my irritation.

Gerald always knew how to poke my buttons; treating me like I didn't know what I was doing was one of them.

"Please send him as soon as possible. My techs will be leaving soon." He looked at my blood-covered arms, his sneer obvious despite the hankie. "Make sure you both clean yourselves up first. It's disgusting in here."

With that, he turned his back on us and left, pulling his booties off as he stepped over the footbath.

As soon as the door closed behind Gerald, Dustin said, "Dr. Richter's one to talk. The microbiology lab smells ten times worse than the necropsy floor. It *always* stinks like musty rot in there. This place will be smelling like roses in about twenty minutes."

Dustin was immensely proud of how he kept the necropsy floor sparkling clean, and he should be; he was damn good at his job.

"I wonder if he goes home smelling like *Staphylococcus* every day," I joked. "We only go home smelling like a dead animal like, what? A day or two a week?"

Dustin flashed me a smile. "A day at most."

We'd get anywhere from one to five carcasses on a regular workday. But thankfully, most of them were fresh and hardly stank at all. Presents like this steer were few and far between, especially when the weather was cooler.

Dustin wrapped a chain around the steer's rear leg. Once secure, the whirl of the electric hoist sounded as the steer rose in the air. I lowered the large necropsy table at the same time. Once the steer's nose cleared the table, Dustin operated the controls to move it into the cooler until the renderer could pick it up. I followed behind him, pushing the offal bin. The renderer came every Friday and would pick up the steer along with the offal bins and other necropsied animals tomorrow.

We worked together to scrub the table clean and wash everything down the drain. With the pleasant smell of the disinfectant filling the air, the stench of the steer was almost entirely chased away.

After the table and floor were washed clean, I washed the blood off my arms and ran a wet paper towel over my face. I started filling out the paperwork to send the samples to the microbiology and virology labs.

Being the only diagnostic laboratory in the state of Oklahoma, we had the full complement of departments on-site: microbiology, virology, serology, PCR, parasitology, toxicology, and pathology. We ran most tests in-house. Sometimes, especially for rare or reportable diseases, we'd have to send samples out to another lab for testing, but that wasn't very often.

I finished the paperwork for the ancillary testing, and Dustin bussed the samples to the appropriate departments, dipping his boots in the footbath as he left. Planning to issue the formal report tomorrow morning, I jotted down a few notes. I also made a quick courtesy call to give the rancher verbal results and left a message. The clock ticked to 4:35 P.M. just as I finished up, and Dustin came back out on the necropsy floor.

"Hope you have fun tonight," Dustin said.

He was standing in the footbath, scrubbing his boots with a long-handled brush. He stepped out when he was done, handing me the brush so I could scrub my own.

"Thanks," I said, trying to keep my voice neutral.

In truth, every time I thought about the date, I was overwhelmed with feelings of dread mixed with hope. I hadn't had the best of luck with relationships lately; I hadn't even gotten so far as a date in the last three months.

"Wash up good," he advised. "Nothin' says 'run away!' more than the smell of a dead animal."

He gave me a cheeky wink and headed into one of two private, all-gender locker rooms before I could reply.

I couldn't help but smile as I headed to the second locker room to change. I took my coveralls off and took a deep sniff. Sure enough, I smelled awful. Like "a dumpster with week-old rotting meat and veggies" awful. I'd have to shower if I wanted to be presentable. I wasn't sure my hair would dry in time but decided wet hair was better than the odor of dead steer.

I took a quick shower in the locker room, sudsing everything up as much as possible. The smell of the tea leaf and mint shampoo filled the locker room. I towel-dried my hair as much as possible before throwing my regular clothes back on.

I dashed back to my office, grateful to see Gerald's door closed as I passed. One brief conversation with the shitass was enough for one day. As I was locking up my office, my phone dinged. I dug it out of my purse to check; it was a text from Wyatt, my date tonight.

This was followed by an emoji of an eggplant and a sweat droplet.

With a sigh, I rolled my eyes and shook my head. *Why do guys have to make everything about sex?* Just another check in the *nope* column.

I shook off the text ick-factor and checked the time on my phone. With a sinking feeling, I realized it was already 5:18 P.M. I only had thirty minutes to run home, change my clothes, and try to do something with my wet hair. Thankfully, I lived a short, ten-minute drive away from anything in Stillwater. With my office locked up, I dashed out of the building to my Prius.

I'd give my date tonight the good ol' college try because Laila would kick my ass if I didn't. But I was not at all optimistic about this match.

CHAPTER
TWO

With about ten minutes to make myself presentable, I pulled into the driveway, hair still wet. Yersi was patiently waiting for me in the front window, folded in an all-black kitty loaf on the windowsill. When I unlocked the front door, his sleek form swirled around my legs, unaware, or uncaring, of the fact that I was frantically trying not to be late for my date. Trying to hustle inside, I side-stepped around him and tossed my purse on the entrance table, accidentally knocking down a huge stack of books waiting to be returned to Aunty. Yersi bolted into the kitchen, spooked.

"Damn it!"

I bent down to push the books to the side so that I could close the front door, feeling each minute slip away. Aunty loved to throw different genres of books at me to see what would stick. This month, she'd gone a little too far with the mysteries, and most would be schlepped back to her unread. My day job *was* mysteries; I wanted to bury myself in fluff fantasy and sci-fi stories during my off time.

As soon as the front door was closed, Yersi let out a reminder yowl from the kitchen. I made a beeline for the fridge and practically threw the wet food in his dish before scrambling to get changed. He let out a *merf* in reply, which could be interpreted as "thanks, most precious human" or, more likely, "about time, servant."

After making sure his royal highness was taken care of, I shucked off my work clothes. Knowing that the dead animal stank had probably seeped into my underwear, I dropped them into the pile, too. Then, I wasted several precious minutes staring stupidly at my closet. It'd been ages since I'd been on a real date, and I had no clue what to wear.

My romantic life, if you could even call it that, pretty much sucked. I'd spent the first eight years of my life dedicated to getting my under-graduate degree and then my DVM. After that, it was three years in a residency program. When most students were out partying and meeting people, I was buried in books, trying to keep my GPA up while working thirty hours a week to put myself through school. Sure, I'd dated people here and there. But, when you're running on empty, there isn't much left to give a love interest.

After passing my board exam and starting my job at the diagnostic lab, I could finally come up to breathe. I'd been working so hard for so long that I almost didn't know what to do in my spare time. Thank-fully, Laila and I met at a new faculty mixer soon after I started, and she'd introduced me to tabletop gaming. Between hanging out with her, cooking, and spending time in my garden, I'd slowly filled up my life with things that brought me joy.

All those experiences meant I was a card-carrying nerd but would eat the dirt when it came to a date.

Which brought me back to my closet—sigh.

What would Wyatt like?

I'd tried to find someone who was just as geeky as I was and would be cool with what I did for a living. It was surprisingly hard to find a person who liked tabletop games *and* was okay with me cutting up dead animals. I had to make some concessions and tweak my profile a bit to finally happen upon Wyatt. Even then, I wasn't so sure about him or dating apps in general, for that matter.

The fact that Wyatt and I didn't share any hobbies should have been a red flag. When he wasn't talking about work, he talked about golf. Golf had always been a rich man's game where I grew up—something they taught at the wealthy, private schools in Edmonton. I didn't even know anyone other than Wyatt who played golf.

Maybe something classy?

But we were going to Eskimo Joe's. I shook my head, chewing on my cheek.

Wyatt also sent emojis that were consistently a little creepy, often of a sexual nature, and misplaced in the text chain. I tried to roll with it; everyone could be socially awkward at times. I probably should've paid attention to that little voice inside that said the guy was not a good fit, but he hadn't balked when I shared that I was a veterinary pathologist. And his pics were cute.

Yeah, probably something casual but sexy.

I picked a cute pair of slinky, deep purple panties and a matching bra; one could always hope. I then scrambled around my closet, trying to find something that wasn't covered in black cat hair. Eventually, I found a pair of clean, fancy jeans that I pulled over my curvy hips, grabbed a fitted shirt to show off my narrow waist, and added a pair of ankle boots.

My hair was still fairly wet and was a tangled mess. I combed it out as much as possible, parted it down the middle, and pulled it into a tidy braid. Makeup was not my thing, and I decided to go *au naturel*. A pair of beaded earrings tied everything together.

After a quick check in the mirror, I sighed. It wasn't my best effort. But it was still pretty damn good for being about an hour away from fishing knee-deep in a bloated, dead steer.

* * *

When I arrived at Eskimo Joe's, the parking situation around the restaurant was a mess. I managed to find a spot about two blocks away and half jogged to the restaurant. Despite good intentions, I was going to be about five minutes late.

When I opened the door, a wave of noise washed over me. The place was fairly busy, with a cacophony of loud chatter and music. Most of the tables were filled, and several people were idling around, waiting to be seated. Trying to catch my breath from the sprint, I looked around for Wyatt.

His polished, dark blue suit stuck out like a sore thumb against the backdrop of t-shirts, cargo shorts, and Crocs. He looked uncomfortable and irritated. I tried to hide the flash of surprise. He'd picked this place; I'd assumed he'd been here before.

Despite him being seriously overdressed, my stomach flopped with instant physical attraction. His suit hugged his upper arms and legs just enough to know that an immaculate body was hidden underneath. His blond hair was trimmed short on the sides and slicked back in a firm, flawless wave on the top. He was clean-shaven and had crystal blue eyes.

He looked up from his phone and caught my eye. Rising from the bench, he wove through the crowd to join me by the door. His smile of recognition fell slightly as his eyes swept over my wet hair and my outfit with vague disappointment.

My back stiffened at the judgment wafting off of him.

Seriously?! We were in Eskimo Joe's, for crying out loud. I was practically over-dressed here. What was he expecting?

"Josie?" he asked, with a hint of doubt in his voice.

"In the flesh. Hope that's not a problem," I replied, unable to hold back the snark. Then, hearing Laila's chiding in my head, I added, "Nice to finally meet you in person."

We awkwardly shook hands and half-hugged in greeting.

He stretched out his arm to expose a fancy watch. "You're a bit late."

Who wears a watch anymore except PE teachers and military personnel? I thought, thrown off by the gesture. *Or is this just another way for him to display his wealth?*

Trying to be polite, I apologized and added, "I ran a tad late at work," hoping he would understand as he was a self-described workaholic.

He smiled slightly, but it didn't reach his eyes.

"I'll grab us a table," he said, stepping back and lifting his hand to catch the host's attention.

Though the place was packed, we were seated immediately. Wyatt and I followed the host and sat across from each other in a booth, the plastic cover squeaking as we scooched in. The host handed us menus and glasses of water before leaving us alone.

I shifted uncomfortably.

Wyatt rested the edge of his hand on the table and then jerked it away, a look of disgust on his face.

"This table is filthy."

Lifting his hand in the air, he snapped his fingers at the nearest server to wave them over.

"Can you please wipe this table down? It's unhygienic."

The server apologized and quickly ran a rag over the table. Mortified, I tried to help, lifting the menus and glasses. Unfortunately, years of heavy dining meant that the cleaning job had left it sticky *and* wet.

Wyatt's frown deepened. A heavy silence spread between us as we looked over the menus, and the noise around us pressed in.

Grasping at straws, I asked, "What are you thinking of ordering?"

"I haven't decided yet. I haven't been here before. I'm thinking of either the Fire Burger or the Bacon and Cheese Burger."

"Their Fire Burger is pretty good," I offered.

"I think I'll get the Bacon and Cheese Burger," he immediately replied, putting the menu down and drinking a sip of water. He looked out at the restaurant, his arms crossed in front of him on the table.

I held the menu higher to hide behind it until the server came. Determined to make the most of the night, I ordered a pulled pork sandwich and fried zucchini; they were my standbys. Ordering something slathered in BBQ sauce may not have been the safest bet for a first date, but I figured this would probably be our first *and* last date. So, fuck it. Feeling extra feisty, I also asked for a chocolate shake.

After our orders were placed, Wyatt resumed his silent observation of the restaurant. I started fidgeting with the piece of paper that had been around the silverware, rolling it tightly, letting it loose, and rolling it again. I kicked myself for not asking Laila to send me a rescue text during the date just in case things went south. I could've used an excuse to leave early.

"How was work today?" I hazarded, grasping for a conversation starter.

Perking up, his eyes shifted back to me and he said, "It was excellent."

Wyatt then embarked on a twenty-minute monologue about finance and how much money he makes. I could only nod and smile, with the occasional *mm-hmm* inserted when he paused to breathe. I'd have preferred sticking toothpicks in my eyes over continuing this one-sided conversation.

I started to zone out.

"Josie? Are you even listening?"

My eyes snapped back to focus, and he leaned back stiffly.

"Huh? Uh, yeah. Up three percent last quarter," I parroted back one of the factoids in his deluge, surprising him.

He pursed his lips, considered me, and took a sip of water just as the server swooped to the rescue, bringing the food.

Grateful to have something to do, I dug into the meal. After clearing half my plate in silence, I asked, "What were you up to last weekend?", trying to coax out more conversation between bites.

"Golf."

"Anything else?"

"No."

Oookay.

"Do you have a group you golf with?"

"Yes."

What the hell?

He'd gone from a solid wall of monologue to monosyllabic answers. I wasn't sure if it was the questions I was asking, the fact that the food was here, or if he had just decided I wasn't worth the effort anymore.

This is a disaster.

Giving up, I let the silence stretch between us as I finished my food. The night wasn't a total loss; the food was tasty. The chocolate shake was nice and thick, the fried zucchini was crunchy, and, though the pulled pork sandwich was dripping in sauce, the bun was still nice and crispy. I even managed to eat everything without getting it all over myself.

As the dishes were cleared, the server asked, "Dessert tonight? Or just the check?"

Before I could answer, Wyatt said, "Just the check, please."

Irritated, I insisted on paying my half when the bill came. I laid out cash for my share plus the tip.

"You did the math wrong," Wyatt splained as he spread the bills out for the tip.

"No. That's thirty percent." *I may not be in finance, but I'm not stupid*, I wanted to add, but I bit it back.

"Tipping thirty percent is ridiculous. The server didn't do anything except write our order down and bring our food when it was already cold."

I stared at him, unable to keep the disdain off my face. The minimum wage for servers in Oklahoma was crap, being less than half the minimum wage for everyone else. Businesses counted on consumers to fill the wage gap, the greedy bastards. Unable to change the system, the least I could do was throw the servers some extra cash in their tip.

Wyatt pushed three dollars over to me.

I'd had just about enough of his crap.

I pushed the bills back and added three more bills to the pile. I swear I heard the theme song of *The Good, The Bad, and The Ugly* whistling through my head. I'd be damned if he won this one.

Seeing my determination, his lips drew into a tight line before he acquiesced. He stiffly stood and put his suit jacket on, buttoning the front. He grabbed my elbow and walked me to the front. Though the touch was gentle, it still felt controlling, and I had to do everything in my power not to shrug him off.

Outside, the silence swept over us as the door shut off the noise. I instantly felt uncomfortable.

I coughed lightly. "Thank you for a nice evening," I said, trying to be polite.

His lips turned up into a smile, but his eyes stayed cool. "My pleasure," he said, voice gravelly.

To my surprise, he leaned over to kiss me.

Good lord, the man thinks he might get some.

I tried not to flinch, hoping I could leave this date with as much grace as possible.

Before his lips could touch mine, he jerked back with a disgusted look on his face. "What is that *smell*?" he said, aghast.

"That's how *my* day went."

I quickly fished my keys out of my purse, squared my shoulders, and turned my back on him. I knew Aunty would be disappointed that I was so rude. But I simply couldn't waste another second on this guy.

Match date: FAIL.

* * *

As I pulled into the driveway, my phone dinged. I sat for a beat, not sure I wanted to check it, and eventually pulled it out of my purse. To my relief, it was a text from Laila; her sixth sense had kicked in again. She always knew when I needed some cheering up.

> How did it go with Wyatt?

I sighed, resting the phone on my leg, thinking about how to respond. Then I typed:

> Yeah...

> What does that mean?

> The guy showed up in a suit and I smelled like dead steer

> You didn't shower?!?!? WTF! You haven't been laid in like a year! He was hot!

> All he did was talk about himself

You don't need to marry the guy SMH

What happened?

> Long story

…

…

Want to have dinner tomorrow?

> Yes! Want to come to my place? I'll cook for you

Sounds good. I'll bring a game to play. What time?

> Six?

She replied with a thumbs up.

I tossed my phone back in my purse.

Screw this dating crap. I'd rather be back at work with a liquified steer than suffer through another date like the one tonight.

I grabbed my stuff and headed inside. Yersi greeted me at the door, rubbing against my legs. I picked him up and scratched his chin. He responded with a purr.

"You're the only man I need, bub."

Merf.

CHAPTER
THREE

I pulled into work Friday morning, grateful to be back in my natural habitat. As I parked my Prius in between two large pick-up trucks, my phone dinged. I turned the car off and dug my phone out of my purse. It was a text from Aunty.

> Good morning sweety. You're on call this weekend right? Are you still coming on Sunday?

> Yes on call but still coming. I wouldn't miss brunch!

She sent a heart emoji in reply.

Aunty wasn't a direct relative, like the sister of one of my parents. But she was my aunt in a distant cousin kinda way. After my mom died, I was pretty much alone without any siblings and a dad who had ghosted before I was born. Aunty stepped up to the plate, becoming my everything: favorite granny, aunty, and best friend bundled into one wonderful person. We had a standing date for brunch on Sunday mornings.

Smiling, I tossed my phone back in my purse.

As I turned to open the car door, I just about crapped my pants when someone banged on the window. Gerald smirked down at me through the passenger side, arm resting on the roof.

"Time for work, Pocahontas," he called through the glass.

Before I could respond, he pounded the roof twice and headed inside.

Fucker.

My heart thudding from the surprise, I took a few deep breaths before I went in. No matter how hard I tried to maintain my serenity around Gerald, the jerk got under my skin every single time.

Once inside the lab, I quickly walked past his open door to my own sanctuary. I had no voicemails and just a couple of emails that I cleared out fairly quickly. With the routine tasks completed, I settled in to write the gross report for yesterday's stinker steer of doom.

After releasing the report, I headed out to the necropsy floor to see if anything had come in overnight. Dustin was already out there, restocking the carts, singing along off-key to "Your Cheatin' Heart."

If I could change one thing about Dustin, it would be his taste in music. I can listen to country music if forced to; you can't live in Oklahoma without being able to. But Dustin insisted on playing Hank Williams and nothing else. Over and over. *All day long.* I'd much rather be listening to hip-hop. But, out of respect for him and his fiefdom, Hank Williams stayed on when we were out on the floor.

I leaned through the door over the footbath.

"Mornin', Dustin," I called out over the music.

"Good mornin', Doc. How'd the date go?"

I made a face, and he started laughing. "That bad, huh?"

"Yeah, it pretty much sucked. Don't even ask."

"Hopefully, it wasn't the stank of the dead steer," he guffawed, not unkindly. "Dolores learned to live with the smell ages ago. She's a keeper."

Being high school sweethearts, Dustin and Dolores had been married for about thirty years. He said the reason they loved each other so much was because they were friends first. They were super cute together, and I was happy for them, even if a bit jealous.

"Anything come in overnight?" I asked.

"There's a suspect parvo puppy. Should be quick and easy. That's it for now."

"'Kay. I'll be right out," I said, nodding slightly.

Dustin was spot on; sadly, puppies dying from parvovirus were very common and routine for us. We'd get so many in that I could practically do the necropsy with my eyes closed—except for the sharp, pointy bits, that is.

I grabbed a lab coat from the rack by the door and slipped into my rubber shoe covers. I dodged the footbath and headed out onto the necropsy floor.

The diagnostic lab's necropsy floor was pretty standard. There were three stainless steel dissection tables arranged in neat rows to the left. A small cart stocked with dissection instruments, formalin jars, and sample collection containers sat beside each table. These small tables were used for dogs, cats, pocket pets, and other small animals. The puppy was already laid out on one of them.

On the far end of the room, there was a large, stainless steel hydraulic table, which was used for the larger animals. The rails for the electric hoist ran over the table and back through the double doors to the cold room. In there, the large animals hung from hooks before and after a necropsy.

A large dissection bandsaw loomed in one corner. This was used for the bigger bones, like the spinal column or limbs of horses. A smaller table-top bandsaw sat on the adjacent counter. That one was used for digits and small pieces of bone.

The room was brightly lit, with additional lamps positioned over the tables that could be turned on as needed. A new layer of epoxy-sealed flooring had just been applied, which made it easy to clean and reduced the slip risk. No one wanted to go ass-over-teakettle with a six-inch blade in their hands.

With the steer long gone, the room was now filled with the familiar scent of cleaning solution; it smelled of sterility. The stainless steel tables glistened. Dustin had done a great job getting everything back in order after yesterday's stank-a-thon.

With practiced ease, I looped my hair around a pen into a tight bun. I loved my hair; it was one of my favorite things about myself. I'd picked my fair share of animal bits and bobs out of my long locks even when tied back, but it was worth it.

Purple nitrile gloves went on with a loud snap.

"Need your knife?" Dustin asked. "I stashed it."

As with most pathologists, I preferred to use my own necropsy knife, which I kept meticulously sharpened. Dustin was pretty good about keeping others away from it, but it would still occasionally get kidnapped despite my last name spelled out in white on the black handle.

"Nah. I'll use a scalpel. Thanks."

The puppy was smaller than a cat. Though I adored my knife, a scalpel was easier to use on the smaller animals. It was safer, too. When I was a resident, one of my mentors insisted that I use a necropsy knife on *everything*, regardless of size. All it took was for me to cut myself doing a snake necropsy, and then I dropped that bit of nonsense. I figured it was about the right tool for the job rather than loyalty to a single instrument.

Grabbing the submission form, I read through the history. The patient was a three-month-old, male Shih Tzu. The owners had brought it home from the breeder about a week ago. The poor guy started having diarrhea a couple of days after that, progressed rapidly, and died. The history was pretty typical, and I agreed with Dustin. Parvoviral infection was the top differential.

The puppy was small enough that I didn't need Dustin's help with the dissection. But he still stayed on hand to pass containers for the samples and label everything once finished. We passed the time talking about what we were going to plant in our veggie gardens this fall when the weather cooled.

After I got everything open, the puppy's intestines were segmentally bright red with a dull, pebbly surface. Thin strands of fibrin stretched across the organs like cobwebs. It was classic for parvoviral enteritis with a possible secondary bacterial infection.

"You called it, Dustin," I said.

He nodded. "I can't remember the last time we got a puppy that *wasn't* parvo."

"I know, right?" I shook my head.

There were a lot of puppy breeders in the region. Some of them were on the up-and-up, but many were puppy mills. The high-density populations combined with an absence of preventative measures, like proper hygiene and vaccinations, made many puppy mills ideal for the spread of the virus.

"Maybe we should talk to Fran about getting the message out again," I suggested. "If people are gonna buy dogs, we might as well educate them on how to find a good breeder."

Dustin shrugged. "You could try, but most people don't care where stuff comes from, even with the animals that they bring home. That's the hard part. Making them care."

I sighed. "Yeah, unfortunately, they don't realize until it's too late." I gestured to the puppy in front of us.

We finished everything up and labeled all of the samples. I ordered virology and microbiology testing on sections of the small intestine to confirm the gross impression. I dropped representative samples in formalin for histology but would hold them. Based on the results from the viral and bacterial testing, I might not need to look at anything under the microscope, and I could save the owner some money by not running any tests I didn't need to.

Once everything was cleaned up, I said, "I'm going to go write this up and get the results out. Just holler if anything else comes in."

"Will do," Dustin said as he headed out with the samples to drop them off in the respective labs.

The virology testing was pretty fast, and I might even know by the end of the day or early tomorrow if parvoviral infection was confirmed. As with most cases, the parvo puppy was pretty cut and dry.

I left the necropsy floor, a bit disappointed at how simple—and preventable—the case had been.

Looking back, I should've been careful mounting that high horse.

* * *

About an hour later, I was in my office finishing up the last bit of paperwork when my desktop phone rang.

"Dr. Harjo. How can I help you?"

"Hey, Doc. We got a gent here with a horse. Dustin's bringing it in. You want to interview him?" It was Anna from the sample receiving department.

"Sure, I'll be right up. Thanks."

I hung up and headed to the interview room.

In Oklahoma, anyone could bring samples to the state diagnostic lab for testing. The people walking in the door ranged from veterinary professionals to owners to animal cruelty investigators. It all depended on the case and what type of testing they needed. The submitted samples were often things like blood, feces, feed, and water. Of course, we also received bodies for necropsy; that was where I came in.

A unique feature of this particular lab was that the pathologist on duty would, if available, interview the submitter. Despite the occasional uncomfortable conversation, I liked it this way. Histories from all of our submitters, veterinarians included, were often tremendously unhelpful. If I could interview folks, I'd be able to get a fuller picture of the situation on the ground and any clinical signs the animal might have exhibited before death. The additional information also helped me understand the extent of the issue and how many other animals might be affected.

The interview room was a small office off the receiving department. It was a typical government room with off-white scuffed walls, buzzing fluorescent lights, a metal desk, and a couple of metal chairs. Faded pet grief counseling and cremation pamphlets sat in a holder on the wall. The room breathed "depressing." I'd brought it up to Fran, but money was tight.

When I walked in with the paperwork, an older man rose from one of the seats, holding his cowboy hat.

I reached out to shake his hand and said, "Hello, I'm Dr. Harjo. Please sit."

"Adam Williams. Thank you, ma'am," he replied with a thick Oklahoma accent.

His hand was large and calloused, and his grip was firm. Sitting back down, he placed his hat next to him. He was a burly man with short gray hair pressed flat on the sides. He wore a neat, crisp, plaid shirt with snap buttons, jeans, and well-worn boots. His bushy eyebrows were pressed together.

I sat down across from him.

He'd only filled out the bare bones on the submittal form. The horse, Shadowhawk, was a thirteen-year-old, gelded Quarter Horse. Other than that, not much information had been provided other than Adam's full name and address along with the business name: JW Ranch.

"Are you Shadowhawk's owner?" I asked to confirm.

"Yes, ma'am."

"Sorry we have to meet like this," I said.

Even though I loved my job, I didn't like all the sadness surrounding it.

"Me, too," Adam said bitterly, looking down at his boots.

I held back the questions to assess his response. At this point, the conversation with an owner could go in one of two directions. In most large animal cases, the interview would proceed matter-of-factly. In other cases, especially with dogs and cats, the tears would start.

He picked up his hat and leaned his arms on his knees with the hat dangling between his legs.

"This is the third one in three days. I can't lose no more," he said gruffly.

My eyes went wide.

"You've lost three horses in three days?" I asked, certain I hadn't heard him right.

"Yes, ma'am. One on Wednesday, one yesterday, and we found Shadowhawk dead this morning."

"I am so sorry," I said, watching his face intently, still not quite over my shock.

"I can't lose no more," he repeated.

He started worrying the edge of his hat with his fingers and chewed at his lower lip.

"Tell me about your ranch. How many horses do you have?" I asked, trying to pull him up from circling the drain.

"We have sixteen horses," Adam answered. He paused to wipe his arm across his forehead. "Well, I guess it's thirteen now."

His right leg started bobbing up and down.

I realized I'd need to ask short, specific questions to tease information out. He was very upset and distracted. I completely understood why; he'd just lost almost a quarter of his herd in a short window of time.

"Are the horses on pasture or in stalls?"

"In stalls," Adam answered quickly.

"Any issues with the waterers?" I probed.

"No, ma'am."

"They all running? You checked them?"

"Yes, ma'am. The ranch hands are supposed to run the waterers each morning when they feed the horses to flush them out. They would'a said something if one of 'em wasn't workin'." His voice wavered slightly.

"Are you on city water or a well?" I asked.

"City water."

I jotted down the info he'd shared. Having a waterer drawing from the city lines made a water-borne disease much less likely. But I still wanted him to bring some of the water in just in case.

"Will you get me a sample of water from Shadowhawk's stall when you get back home?" I asked. "You can just put it in a plastic bottle or a jar. That way, we have a sample from the day he passed."

Adam nodded, leg still bobbing and fingers running the rim of his hat.

"What do you use for feed?" I continued.

"All the horses get alfalfa daily. We also give them pelleted feed."

"Do they all get the same feed? Any treats?" I probed.

"Yes, ma'am. The ranch hands feed them all the same thing. My wife will occasionally feed them apples or carrots."

"See any beetles or odd weeds or plants in alfalfa?"

Blister beetles were fairly common in Oklahoma, and if the alfalfa was heavily infested, something like that could take out a couple of horses in just a few days. The nasty critters were small black beetles about the length of the tip of a thumb and were usually pretty easy to spot in the alfalfa or out in a heavily infested field.

"No, the alfalfa is good stuff," he answered with a hint of defensiveness. "Been using the same guy for over fifteen years."

I nodded. It could still be blister beetles, but I kept that to myself. I didn't want to worry Adam or cast any doubt on his supplier. I'd still be looking for any gross lesions associated with blister beetle ingestion and checking the stomach contents for any bug parts.

"What about the pelleted feed?" I asked.

"It's good stuff, too. It's Best in Class. Been feeding that for years now," he replied.

It was a brand I didn't recognize, which wasn't a huge surprise; everyone was trying to edge into the pet food market these days. Regardless of whether I knew the brand or not, we needed a sample of that, too.

"Can you bring some of that by, as well? You can fill a one-gallon Ziplock baggie with it. We'll only test it if we need to. I just want to make sure we a sample before you start opening new bags."

"Yes, ma'am. Should we stop feeding them the pellets?" he asked, looking up at me, brow crinkled.

"Wouldn't hurt. Make sure to triple-check the alfalfa, too. I wouldn't throw anything away yet. Just hold onto it for a couple of days until we can figure out what's going on. After you take your water sample, you might also want to clean out the waterers and flush the system. I think something in the water is less likely, but better safe than sorry."

I made some quick notes before asking, "Did any of the horses look sick or act unusual before they died?"

"The first two we found dead in their stalls. One of 'em looked like he thrashed a bit. The wood shavings were all pushed around. After that, we would go out and check on them every few hours, even through the night. Early this morning, Shadowhawk was rolling on the ground in his stall. Doc Anderson came over as soon as we called, but

Shadowhawk was dead before he got there. He said I needed to bring him in right away."

The thrashing was a fairly non-specific clinical sign. It could be anything from colic to neurological disease. It was still worth noting, and I jotted that on the form.

"Is this Dr. Anderson from Willow Park Mobile Vet?" I asked.

He nodded.

"Are you okay with me speaking with Dr. Anderson and sending a copy of the results to him?"

The submitter essentially owned the results. Just like human medical records, we needed permission to share test results with anyone else.

Adam nodded his consent. I added the veterinarian's information to the submittal form.

"I'll give Dr. Anderson a call right after we're finished talking and make sure he stays informed. Are any of the other horses sick?"

Adam shook his head. "Doc took a look at the others and said they seemed okay."

"Any of them wobbly, not wanting to eat, acting differently?"

"No, ma'am."

"Any diarrhea or coughing?"

He shook his head again, and he drew his lips into a tight, thin line.

I made a few more notes on the form. Most pathologists didn't like the term "sudden death." All death was *technically* sudden. The clinical signs an animal had before it died could point a pathologist in one direction or another. But these horses died with little to no observed clinical signs. All bets were off in this case.

Trying to dig out more information, I asked, "Are they vaccinated and dewormed?"

"Yes, ma'am," Adam replied.

I couldn't help feeling like all of my questions were irritating him, but I pressed on anyway.

"What are they vaccinated for?"

He looked up at the ceiling, trying to remember. "I'd have to check. We just do what the doc says."

"Not a problem. I'll ask Dr. Anderson about the vaccines." I added notes about the lack of other clinical signs.

Adam hadn't given me much to go on. Given that I might be dealing with neurological disease, viral infection was high up on the differential list, and it was important to know what the horses had been vaccinated for. I was already starting to build a differential list in my head and was feeling the itch to get started on the necropsy. These kinds of cases kept things exciting, and I was looking forward to getting Adam an answer and saving the rest of the herd.

Adam cleared his throat and, looking down at the floor, he said, "This may not be important. But we did have a ranch hand leave recently."

I looked up, trying to make eye contact. His gaze stayed down on the floor, brows furrowed and leg bobbing up and down. He swiped his hand through his hair.

"Tell me more," I nudged, trying to keep my voice neutral.

It always amazed me how little faith people had in their fellow human beings. Invariably, if a death was a surprise, they were always pointing a finger at their neighbor or an angry ex. In reality, the animal usually died from cancer or an infection that had gone unnoticed. This blame game happened so often that it was a running joke around the lab. When interviewing an owner, however, I tried to keep a straight face and just take notes.

"He didn't show up for work a few days in a row. And he was always smokin' in the barn. My wife ain't havin' none of that. It's too dangerous. We both talked to him a couple of times. About a week ago, he got in a shouting match with her, pushed her into a wall, and took off. The horses started dying a few days later."

Now, that's *different.*

"How was he with the horses?" I asked, my interest now piqued.

"Didn't seem to care about 'em. If he ever showed up, he'd do the work. But he didn't have a way with them. Know what I mean? Or the cattle neither."

I knew exactly what he was talking about. As soon as someone was around an animal, you could tell how they felt about them. Body language and the animal's response said oodles. But it didn't mean the guy would go so far as to whack one of them.

"Any reason to suspect the ranch hand might have done something malicious?"

He shrugged. "Just don't know." There was an odd, almost smug inflection in his response that confused me.

I studied him closely. He was still hunched over, arms resting on his knees and looking at the ground. The cowboy hat continued to spin in his hands.

"You have cattle, too? Do the ranch hands take care of them, as well?"

"Yes, ma'am. We have about fifty head. They're out on pasture. The hands usually don't work with them much." Adam chewed on his cheek.

"Are any of the cattle or other animals sick or dead on the farm? No dead birds or anything?"

"No, ma'am."

I was running out of questions. The submittal form was covered in notes, but none of them were very helpful. I felt like the additional history I'd teased out of him had only narrowed the list of possible causes ever so slightly. In contrast to the puppy that screamed "parvo" before I even opened it, there was a long laundry list of things that could have killed this horse. I needed to get the horse open to figure out what was going on.

This is gonna be a weird one, I thought as I forced a confident smile to reassure him.

"I think I have what I need for now. If you think of anything else, just give me a call. You can call the main line and ask for Dr. Josie Harjo. Did they give you your accession number?"

"Yes, ma'am." He patted the pocket of his shirt.

I stood, and Adam followed, placing his hat on his head. We shook hands.

"We'll figure this out, Mr. Williams. In the meantime, don't forget to collect the water and feed to bring in. Dr. Anderson will likely have some other ideas on how to protect the rest of your horses until we get an answer."

After a beat, and against my better judgment, I added, "And, just to be safe, it wouldn't hurt to keep that ranch hand off your property until we figure this out."

CHAPTER
FOUR

Eager to get cracking on the case, I saw Adam out and passed the completed submittal form back to Anna in the receiving department. There were a few things that needed to be sorted before I could get started.

I poked my head out on the necropsy floor. Dustin had already used the hoist to pull the horse out of the trailer and lay it on its left side on the hydraulic necropsy table. The *shick, shick, shick* of him straightening the edge of his knife could be heard over the predictable Hank Williams.

"Hey, Dustin," I called out.

The sound of the knife on the steel stopped, and Dustin looked up. He laid the instruments down and headed over to the door.

"What's the story?" he asked.

"It's a neuro horse."

Dustin frowned and sighed. "Well, that sucks."

"Yeah, I know," I said sympathetically, fully aware of how much of a PITA it was to pull the spinal cord out of a horse.

"Rabies protocol?" he asked.

Two things could stop a necropsy dead in its tracks: rabies and anthrax. If either one was on the differential list, we couldn't open the animal until that was ruled out. With anthrax, we could just take a quick blood sample, run it down the hall, and get an answer in about fifteen minutes. Rabies was a whole other bag of beans. If rabies was a solid differential, we'd have to fully gown up, remove the brain, and ship a section to the state for testing. The body would then have to sit in the cooler—and continue to rot—for a few days until the negative result came back.

"I don't think it's rabies. Three horses have died within the last few days." I chewed the inside of my cheek, considering.

Rabies cases were pretty rare; one or two a year would come into the lab. So, the chances were super low to begin with. On top of that, rabies cases were typically one-offs. I'd never seen them cluster like this before. There'd have to be a rabid coyote or something running loose in the barn, getting into the stalls and biting the horses.

"Let me call the vet and see if the horses were vaccinated. I'll be right back."

Dustin nodded. He was a little more lackadaisical than me and would be just fine cutting into the body right now. But he also knew it was *my* neck on the line if the horse ended up popping positive.

I was crossing my fingers and toes that the horse was vaccinated and that the vet didn't think it was rabies. With a mortality rate at almost twenty percent already, we couldn't just let the body hang in the cooler for three days, waiting for the state to get back to us with a rabies result. We needed answers soon, or more horses were going to die.

From my office, I gave the vet a jingle. I knew Dr. Charlie Anderson well, and we were on a first-name basis. He'd been running his mobile vet service for over forty years and was past retirement age. He was damn good at his job and had a way with people. Most ranchers didn't want to pay for a necropsy, but Charlie did an excellent job of showing them the value of it. Because of that, we crossed paths fairly often.

"Willow Park Mobile Vet. How may I help you?" the receptionist answered.

"Hello, this is Dr. Josie Harjo from the diagnostic lab. Is Dr. Anderson available? I'm calling about Shadowhawk Williams."

"Howdy, Dr. Harjo. Dr. Anderson is doing farm visits. Would you like his cell?"

I took down the number on a sticky note, thanked the receptionist, and dialed Charlie's cell. He answered on the fourth ring, shouting into the phone over the sound of a large tractor.

"Hey, Charlie, this is Josie from the diagnostic lab. Do you have a sec to talk about Shadowhawk? The horse from JW Ranch?"

"Dr. Harjo! Thanks for calling. Let me step inside my truck so I can hear you better." There was a long pause, the slam of a door, and Charlie came back on the line sans the tractor noise. He continued, "That's better. Did you say they brought in the horse from JW Ranch?"

"Yes, sir. Just now."

"I am glad they did. It took some convincing. Honestly, they should've called me after the first one died. I don't know why they waited so long. Real sad what happened out there, and I think more could go. Odd situation."

"I'm glad they brought it in, too. I want to get the horse opened up today, but I need to make sure rabies isn't on the differential list."

Please, please, please tell me you aren't worried about rabies.
"Well, I'm pretty sure the patient was seizing before it died, and ya always gotta have rabies on the list with a neuro horse."

Dang it.

"Yes, I know, I know," I answered, pretending to be resigned, and then added hopefully, "But have you ever seen rabies take out three horses?"

"No, ma'am."

"Are the horses on the ranch vaccinated for rabies?"

"Let me check. I got my laptop right here." The sounds of him shuffling around filled the space until he spoke again. "Looks like they've all had rabies shots. They've also had West Nile and equine encephalitis shots along with herpes, tetanus, rhino, and flu."

I'll admit, I did a slight fist pump. I might get a verbal ass-chewing from my boss, but I was getting this horse opened today.

"Mr. Williams said the horses had almost no clinical signs prior to death. What did he tell you?"

"Same thing," Charlie replied. "I looked over the rest of the horses, and they all seemed fine."

"Did you see the other dead horses? Did they have any bites or signs of trauma?"

"They buried them with the backhoe before I arrived," he said with a slight huff.

My eyebrows creased. "That's weird. And they didn't call you until Shadowhawk started showing signs?"

He grunted and said, "Yes, ma'am. Those're expensive horses. He does competitive barrel racing and has won several titles. He should've called me when the first one died."

"How valuable are the horses? He didn't mention insurance." I started twiddling my pen. This case was all over the place.

"I'm almost certain they're insured." Sounds of typing came through the phone, and then he said, "Yep, all insured."

"Funny he didn't put that on the paperwork," I mused. "Do you know if a necropsy report is required to collect the payout?"

Insurance policies on valuable horses often ran in the millions. A few forms needed to be filled out for the claims. Sometimes, the veterinarian just had to confirm the identity and death of the animal, which would be Charlie's job. Other times, a full necropsy report was required, which would fall to me. Most owners were on top of that and let us know up-front. There was even a section on the submittal form asking about insurance; it helped remind them and streamlined the process. I could only guess that Mr. Williams was in so much shock that he neglected to fill out that part of the form.

"I don't know 'bout the JW Ranch policy," Charlie said. "I'll look into it and get back to you on whether they'll need the necropsy report. Not sure how to handle the other two horses he already buried."

I could practically see him shaking his head in disappointment. It was hard to sign a form saying an animal was dead if you hadn't seen it.

"Mr. Williams mentioned an angry employee. Did he say anything to you?" I asked.

"Mr. Williams didn't," he grunted. "But his wife sure gave me an earful. She's pretty convinced the ranch hand is somehow involved."

"Do you think he's involved?" I asked, still doubtful.

"No, ma'am." He echoed my thoughts and huffed a laugh. "You know how it is. Everyone thinks the guy next door poisoned their dog, and it ends up being a cardiac hemangiosarcoma that ruptured."

I felt myself nodding, even though he couldn't see me. "What are your differentials?"

He let out a frustrated sigh. "The water looked clean. The bales looked nice. The other horses seemed fine. If it was just one, I said an intestinal torsion or something. But three—that's quite a bit. I've seen outbreaks of herpesvirus like this, but the horses at JW Ranch are vaccinated. Since they're all in stalls with good quality alfalfa, I'm scratching my head."

I felt a tad better knowing that Charlie was also stumped.

"Yeah, I think herpesvirus is still on the list. I'll still check for it. But, knowing they're vaccinated, there's a long list of odd-ball differentials at this point."

I tapped my pen on the desk, racking my brain for any more questions before I let Charlie go. Unable to think of anything else, I said, "I think that's it for now. Thank you for your time, Charlie. Since rabies seems pretty unlikely, I'm going to go ahead and do the full necropsy today. I'll still have to send the brain to the state. And I'll have to hold the other samples until it comes back negative. But I can check for some obvious stuff on gross and get samples in formalin. The gross report should be out by end-of-day."

"Thank you kindly, Josie. Appreciate it."

"No problemo," I said warmly. "If you talk to Mr. Williams, please remind him to bring the feed and water in."

* * *

Dressed in coveralls and rubber boots, I headed back out onto the necropsy floor, a tight knot of apprehension starting to build in my gut. Despite my love of the profession, the pressure of those thirteen living horses left at JW Ranch loomed over me. It was my job to make sure no more of them died, and I felt the weight of every single life.

I splashed through the footbaths out onto the floor.

Let's do this.

"So?" Dustin asked casually.

"Survey says cut 'er open. The horses are vaccinated, and with multiple animals dead, rabies is unlikely. We should still collect a section of the brain and send it to the state."

"Roger that," he replied.

I was taking a very slight risk pushing forward with the necropsy before the rabies results were back. But the chances of this horse having rabies were slim to none, and everyone in the lab was vaccinated. No one would get sick if the horse was positive. I'd just get a hefty slap on the wrist, everyone would have to get blood drawn for rabies titers, and I'd have to do a crap ton of paperwork if the horse tested positive.

Dustin wet down the necropsy table and the floor beneath, leaving the hose running. The necropsy table had a large lip around ninety percent of the edge that kept the blood from spilling over the edges and directed it to a spillway over the drain in the floor. Wetting down the surfaces and leaving the hose running near the drain kept the blood from sticking and made the post-necropsy cleanup a heck of a lot easier.

I walked around the horse to complete the external exam. I took pictures of the horse's facial markings; they might be important for the insurance. There were no other identifying markers, like a lip tattoo or brand on the rump, which I noted on the form.

The skin was abraded along the left rear leg, and the tissue beneath was dark red with bruising, likely from the thrashing. I snapped a quick picture of it, even though I wasn't too concerned. Other than that, there were no other outward signs of trauma to suggest an animal bite or something more nefarious. Though the lack of a visible bite mark didn't rule out rabies on its own, it added another notch to the "unlikely to be rabies" column.

The horse's jaw was firmly closed with rigor, its tongue trapped between its teeth. I pulled back the lips, checking for any ulcers or other lesions. Everything was squeaky clean.

Dustin, always anticipating my next move, handed me a syringe. I drew some aqueous humor from the eye. I injected the clear, sticky fluid into a red top tube, dropped the syringe into the sharps bin, and handed the tube to Dustin to label. Aqueous humor wasn't a common sample type, but it was useful for measuring some trace mineral concentrations. Plus, in cases where I had no flipping clue what was going on, I was a firm believer in collecting everything and saving it should the samples be needed later. Once the body went off to the renderer, there were no take-backsies.

I grabbed my knife. Dustin held up the front leg for me as I stabbed the skin in the axillary area, making a C-shaped cut to reflect the leg. Dustin pulled it back to the opposite side of the table with a crackling sound. I grabbed another tube, collecting some of the blood that leaked out from the axillary vessels. It was semi-clotted but still useful for some tests, like looking for viral antibodies.

I moved to the rear of the horse, stabbing the knife in the groin to reflect the back leg, cutting through the ligament in the hip joint with a popping sound. I then peeled back the skin over the abdomen and made a C-shape cut along the edge of the ribs and toward the back, letting the abdominal muscles flop forward.

Before I started mucking around in the abdomen, I took a quick look to make sure everything was in the right place. Horse guts had a habit of floating to the wrong side of the abdomen, twisting around other loops, and getting trapped in places. Though I was hoping for a torsion or some other intestinal issue, the gastrointestinal tract looked peachy keen. In my heart of hearts, I knew it wouldn't be a GI thing, but I was still disappointed.

I was delighted to find the urinary bladder full, which often wasn't the case. Urine was an important sample to test for toxins, and I wasn't always lucky enough to find any urine left to collect. Many animals pissed themselves when they died. And it sounded like the horse might have been seizing before it had passed, which often made animals lose bladder control. In a case like this, the more samples, the merrier.

"Can you grab me a urine cup?" I asked.

Dustin handed me the cup. I pressed it against the bladder and made a small stab above the opening. Bright yellow urine quickly filled it to the brim. I screwed the blue cap on and handed it over to Dustin to label.

"Let's get all of this out," I said, eager to start working my way through the other organ systems. Surely, there had to be a lesion somewhere; I just had to find it.

I cut through the diaphragm with a whoosh of air and, with Dustin's help, chomped through the ribs with the loppers. The thoracic cavity also looked crystal clear, with the pink, fluffy lungs hugging the heart.

"Ain't much there," Dustin mused.

"Yeah, there's *nothing* there, unfortunately," I huffed.

I chewed on the inside of my cheek as I noodled over the case, secretly hoping that I didn't totally screw the pooch and brazenly expose us both to rabies.

With both cavities open, we started going through the familiar motions of removing all of the organs. The endless loops of intestine *schlooped* onto the floor, splashing me with partially digested feed. Dustin laughed in sympathy; we'd all been there. At least I didn't get any in my mouth, which, sadly, had happened to both of us more than once.

I laid the gastrointestinal tract out on the floor, slicing through the mesentery with my knife. Squatting over the stomach, I made an incision along the greater curvature. Inside, there were clumps of soft, chewed feed that had a slightly sour, earthy smell. I pinched through the contents, looking for anything out of place. Digging through the stomach contents was one way to confirm blister beetle toxicity in horses during the gross examination.

"Find anything?" Dustin asked as he pulled the pluck out, placing the tongue, esophagus, trachea, lungs, and heart on a large dissection table in one piece.

"Nope. No beetles. And no ulcers in the oral cavity."

Even though I didn't find anything suspicious, I decided to collect some of the stomach contents. Something was bugging me about the angry ranch hand, and I didn't want to brush it off. The toxicology lab could always test the stomach contents later if we needed to go down that route.

I gently rinsed the inside of the stomach with water. About a half-dozen botfly larvae were attached to the inner layer, an extremely common finding in horses. Though botfly larvae weren't symbiotic parasites, colonization of the stomach was a benign process in horses, and I wasn't worried about them in the slightest. Other than the larvae, the stomach was frustratingly normal.

"The mucosa of the stomach looks good," I added.

The lack of irritation to the stomach made blister beetle toxicity even more unlikely. It also ruled out a couple of other gastric irritants.

I quickly ran the rest of the gastrointestinal tract, collecting representative samples to plop in the formalin bucket. Once finished, I stood, knife still in hand, staring down at the GI tract and chewing the inside of my cheek.

Dustin, sensing my worry, started singing along to "Honky Tonk Blues" to lighten the mood. I couldn't fight the smile. He danced a bit as we worked together to load the loops of intestine into the offal bin.

With the GI tract completed, I worked my way through the remaining abdominal organs as my heart continued to sink. I bread-loafed the liver, cutting evenly spaced sections and pinching them between my fingers. Everything looked and felt normal. I did the same thing with the spleen. Moving onto the kidneys, I cut each one in half length-wise. They also looked completely normal.

As a pathologist, we live by lesions. Diseased organs were our bread and butter. So far, I hadn't found a damn thing, and it was weighing heavy on me. I tried to wave off the disappointment by going through the motions of sample collection. Small, representative sections of each organ were dropped into formalin for histology. Fist-sized portions of fresh liver and kidney were harvested to freeze for toxicology.

"Hey, Dustin. Can you grab some CSF?" I called out just as Dustin was getting ready to cut the horse's head off.

"Got you," he answered.

He grabbed a syringe and drew the cerebral spinal fluid through the ventral surface of the atlanto-occipital joint. The fluid was clear and looked completely normal.

"Nothing?" I asked.

"Nope," he confirmed.

"Save it just in case."

"Roger."

He squirted the CSF into a red top tube and dropped the syringe in the sharps bin.

"Maybe wear a mask when you do the brain and spinal cord?" I suggested.

Dustin gave me a look, one eyebrow cocked.

"I know. Do it for me?" I threw him a playful begging look.

Being a seasoned veteran on the necropsy floor, he often took risks I wasn't always comfortable with. The last thing I wanted was to try to explain to his partner why he died from something he picked up on the floor because he wasn't wearing the correct personal protective equipment.

Dustin shrugged and obliged by putting on a mask, face shield, and arm covers.

I moved over to the pluck, running the knife down the esophagus and then the trachea. The lungs palpated normally: delicate, soft, and slightly crepitus. I bread-loafed the lungs as well in case I'd missed something on palpation but was disappointed. Samples of lung bobbed in the formalin, floating to the surface. I dissected the heart, opening the right side with a C-shape and the left side with a straight cut down the middle. Once again, everything looked normal.

By the time I had finished mucking around the lungs and heart, Dustin had already disarticulated the head. It was sitting in a clamp, skin removed and flaps hanging to the sides. Using a hacksaw, he artfully cut through the skull without even nicking the brain. He was a frigging CNS *ninja*. After delicately removing the brain from the calvarium, he collected the samples for rabies testing in a petri dish to send to the state and sealed it with parafilm.

"Want any fresh?" he asked.

I was busy labeling samples and walked over to look at the brain. It looked normal, like everything else in the horse. I chewed the inside of my cheek, now raw and sore, frustrated.

"Yes, please. We'll need it for virology," I answered.

He took a section of the brain and laid it in a second petri dish, sealing it with parafilm. He double-bagged it in Ziplock bags with a biohazard symbol and marked it as a rabies suspect. The rest of the brain was plopped in a large bucket of formalin.

Using the hoist, he went about disarticulating the horse. Once he had the spinal column isolated, he ran it on the bandsaw and then teased the spinal cord out. I did a once-over of the cord before he put it in the formalin fixative.

"For such a dramatic history, this is the most boring necropsy ever," I said with some bitterness.

I was dreading the gross report, which would be about all of three, unhelpful sentences. I had zero answers and felt guilty about it. As the pathologist on the case, it was my job to come up with an answer, and I felt empty-handed.

"Meh," Dustin said, shrugging. "It is what it is."

We set about labeling all of the samples as "rabies suspect" and double-bagged them. The stomach contents, liver, kidney, aqueous humor, brain, and CSF went in a special rabies suspect box in the freezer. The urine and the blood were kept in a small rabies suspect tub in the fridge. The formalin jars stayed on a separate cart. We wouldn't be able to take anything off the necropsy floor until the brain came back negative for rabies, no matter how eager I was to get answers. Rules were rules. At the end of the day, those rules usually saved lives.

"If the rabies comes back negative…." I caught myself. "*When* the rabies comes back negative, let's get that brain to virology for herpes and West Nile testing."

"Roger that," Dustin said, nodding slightly.

Ever the optimist, I filled out the virology paperwork and tucked it next to the frozen brain.

We worked in sync to scrub everything down, the strong scent of disinfectant spreading through the room. Dustin spent extra time on the bandsaw and the clamp, washing the flecks of bone and muscle down the drain and dousing the equipment with dilute bleach to kill anything that might be left behind.

I stared at the tendrils of blood mixing with water, thoughts whirling. We'd ruled out a lot during the necropsy: traumatic injury, blister beetles, intestinal disease, and more. But a long list of possibilities remained, and thirteen more horses were counting on me to figure this mess out.

CHAPTER
FIVE

After all evidence of the horse was washed away from the necropsy floor, I changed back into my civvies and headed back to my office. I knew the gross report would be irritatingly unhelpful, and I was agitated.

During my residency, we were taught that ruling things out was just as important as finding the cause of death. That mantra always kinda irked me; it was an ivory-tower view to make pathologists feel better about not knowing what the fuck was going on. There wasn't an owner or a vet who liked to read "within normal limits" in a report. They wanted answers and, sometimes, needed those answers urgently. They simply couldn't wait a month or more for a pathologist to suss out a case.

As expected, the Shadowhawk report was only a handful of sentences long, consisting mainly of a description of the horse's markings for insurance purposes. I tried to add some padding to the comment, outlining all of the things I was confident in ruling out, like gastrointestinal torsion and trauma. There were so many differentials left on the list that I didn't bother listing them all out. Instead, I ended the report with a vague reference to additional testing that was pending.

With an inward cringe, I released the report. At this particular diagnostic lab, we released results to whomever submitted the case. The submitter could be the owner, the veterinarian, or even a Department of Food and Agricultural employee. This process had its pluses and minuses. The upside was that owners who didn't have a veterinarian could get access to the diagnostic testing they needed for their animals. It also gave us an opportunity to encourage the owner to get the help of a vet.

There were also some pretty big downsides to letting anyone off the street bring samples in. The biggest downside to releasing results to owners was that most of them didn't know how to interpret the scientific report. It wasn't a matter of intelligence; it had more to do with whether or not they knew the scientific language we had to use in our reports. Unless I tossed in some clear verbiage, I'd most assuredly get a call from the owner requesting an explanation as to what everything meant. I'd learned early on to proactively call owners in all but the most clear-cut cases. Unless it was "yes, Fluffy had lymphoma," I'd be picking up the phone.

In this case, there was no easy way to say that I had no clue what was going on. Charlie had been a vet long enough that he'd seen his fair share of reports like this. But I knew Mr. Williams was going to have questions, and they'd be ones I couldn't answer just yet.

I begrudgingly picked up the phone to call Shadowhawk's owner.

A masculine voice answered on the second ring. "Hello, this is Adam."

"Hello, Mr. Williams. This is Dr. Harjo from the diagnostic lab. I'm calling about Shadowhawk."

"Hello," he replied gruffly. "What'd you find?"

I found the shit-sandwich method was the best for delivering news like this. I dove right in.

"We were able to rule several things out. I didn't see any signs of trauma. There was no intestinal torsion or blockage, and I didn't find any evidence of blister beetles."

He huffed. "I coulda told you it wasn't blister beetles. I've been going to the same guy for my feed for fifteen years."

Pressing on, I said, "I still don't know the cause of death yet. I've collected several samples, but I have to wait until the rabies results come back before I can do any more testing."

"Rabies?" he interrupted, skepticism apparent in his tone.

"It's more a precaution than anything else," I continued. "I honestly don't think it's rabies. But I think Shadowhawk may have had seizures before he passed. For safety reasons, I have to run a rabies test before I send the other samples out."

He grunted.

"It's to protect the employees in the lab," I added, trying to appeal to his altruistic side, if he even had one. There was something about Adam that was rubbing me the wrong way.

He grunted again and asked, "How long is that rabies test gonna take?"

I cringed inwardly. There wasn't much I could do at this point; I was equally frustrated that there was nothing obvious on the gross examination. We'd have to wait days, maybe even longer, before we had an answer. And, heaven forbid, there was even a chance we might not figure it out at all; those types of cases were awful.

"We'll probably get the rabies results back early next week," I answered cautiously. Some owners could get mighty feisty if they had to anxiously wait through a weekend for results.

After a beat, he asked, "Then what?"

"Once we get the rabies results back, I'll test for herpesvirus to be safe. I've seen herpes do this before, but Dr. Anderson confirmed that your horses are vaccinated for EHV. If that comes back negative, we'll have to wait until I can look at everything under the microscope before I get a better idea of what's going on."

An uncomfortable silence stretched between us for a beat, so I rambled on, "It usually takes about a week to look at things under the microscope. But I'll try to push it through faster if I can. I know you're worried about your other horses, and I'm doing everything within my power to get you an answer as soon as possible." After an awkward pause, I added, "How're the other horses doing?"

"Haven't lost any more today," he answered curtly.

"That's great news," I said, trying to be hopeful.

"Are you testing for poison?" he asked. "I'm sure Ben did something."

"Ben?" I asked, confused.

"The ranch hand," he said, agitated. "I'm sure he did something. We've got all sorts of stuff around the ranch he coulda used."

My brow furrowed, and I started tapping my pen. Usually, these were pretty quick, polite calls, even if I could hear disappointment in an owner's voice. Adam was pushing me, and it set my teeth on edge.

I continued carefully. "Have you seen him around the ranch?"

"No, ma'am," he said, full-on irritated now. "Not since we fired him. But it's a big place. I bet he snuck in at night and poisoned them. Sue's sure it's him. That bastard better not show his face around here."

My level of concern was increasing rapidly. The last thing I wanted was for this guy to grab his shotgun and shoot his former employee. I tried to talk him down.

"It's extremely rare for an animal to be maliciously poisoned." I was careful to avoid saying that it never happened.

"Are you going to submit a sample to check for poisoning or not?"

Now, his voice sounded nervous. I was still scrambling to figure this dude out. By his tone, I couldn't tell if he wanted me to find something to pin on the ranch hand, Ben, or if he was scared that I would send the samples in for toxicology testing.

Trying to keep my voice neutral and logical, I answered, "With toxicology, we have to know what we're looking for. There's no single test that can tell me if Shadowhawk was poisoned or not. I'll need to look at the tissues under the microscope first. Otherwise, we could spend a ton of money testing for everything under the sun, and they could still all come back negative."

His silence echoed on the other end of the line.

I chewed the inside of my cheek, trying to figure out the best way through this conversation. I decided to give him a to-do; that might help calm him down.

"If you haven't yet, please bring the water and the feed to the lab. We can examine that while we wait for the rabies results."

"Yes, ma'am," he replied coolly.

"I wish I had more for you. I'll call you as soon as I do."

After stilted goodbyes, the call ended.

I rested the phone down with a sinking feeling in the pit of my stomach. I was already feeling a bit dodgy about this case, and the call only made it worse. Adam was acting squirrelly. Something was off, and I couldn't put my finger on it. I'd just have to wait and hope no more horses died while I was trying to sort this mess out.

* * *

It was already getting late in the workday, and I wanted to pick Sandy's brain before everyone checked out for the weekend.

Dr. Sandy Bishop was head of the toxicology department and was the most badass veterinary toxicologist in the country. Oklahoma had a wealth of poisonous plants and critters. The weather was perfect for cooking blue-green algae in ponds and just humid enough to grow mold in feed. The over-farming and manic climate also led to mineral deficiencies in some pastures and toxic concentrations of compounds, like nitrates, in others. All of these factors made the Oklahoma state diagnostic lab the perfect place to learn anything and everything about veterinary toxicology. The entire lab, and the state, for that matter, was dreading the day Dr. Bishop would retire.

I lightly knocked on Sandy's door. "Dr. Bishop?"

"I'm here. Come on in," a pleasant voice called out.

I let myself into the cramped office. Piles of books, papers, and files sat on every surface. Despite the clutter, it was an ordered chaos. Sandy could magic a relevant article from one of the many mountains of papers without even having to hunt for it; I'd seen her do it. She'd be like, "Oh, there's a paper on that from 1986," and *poof*! She'd drop it in my hand. I never understood how she kept track of everything or could even remember a case report from almost forty years ago.

Sandy was seated at her desk, reading glasses perched on her nose, peering closely at her computer screen and poking at the keyboard. She was in her early sixties and heavy-set with dark brown skin and short, gray, curly hair.

As I sat down, Sandy peered over the top of her reading glasses and turned to me.

"How can I help you, Josie?" she asked.

"I got a weird one for you." I sat down across from her, unable to prevent a frustrated huff from escaping.

"I love weird. Bring it." She grinned and leaned back in her chair.

"The case came in today. Thirteen-year-old, male Quarter Horse. Three horses have died over the last three days, and there are thirteen left."

Her eyebrows went up, and she let out a low whistle.

"Yeah, I know," I said, frowning slightly in sympathy. "The horses are kept in stalls on city water. They get alfalfa and pelleted feed. There are also cattle on the farm, and they're fine, but they're out on a separate pasture. Charlie Anderson from Willow Park—he's been out there. He didn't see any of them sick before they died. But, from the way the owner talks, I think they might be having seizures or be in pain right before they die."

Sandy started rocking her chair gently, hands resting in her lap as she listened.

"And I know what you're thinking. Has to be EHV, right? But the horses are vaccinated."

"Huh," Sandy said, pursing her lips.

"The horse was squeaky clean on necropsy."

"You're naughty, Dr. Harjo. You know you shouldn't have cut that horse up until the rabies results came back," she chided, not unkindly.

Chagrinned, I replied, "Yeah. But the risk was super low, and I was really hoping I'd find something. I didn't want the horse to rot in the cooler over the weekend."

Sandy leaned forward and rested her elbows on the desk. "And you wanna help the other horses. I get it." She shrugged, signaling her understanding.

"Any ideas? I plan on testing for EHV and West Nile, just in case. I know histo will help narrow things down, but that's gonna take a while. I can always send out for the encephalitides later if the histo looks like it might be viral."

"I think you're on the right track ruling out viral disease first, especially herpes. If you hear hoofbeats, think of horses, not zebras. It's probably not protozoal myelitis either with so many horses dead." Sandy took off her reading glasses, letting them dangle on their chain. She rubbed her eyes, brow furrowed in thought.

"Because they're on automatic waterers, blue-green algae is unlikely. Do they have salt blocks? Are all the waterers working?" she asked.

"Not sure about salt blocks. But, according to the owner, the waterers are working," I answered.

"Probably not salt toxicity, anyway," she mused, waving her hand dismissively.

"I have CSF saved in case we need to test for it," I replied. "I asked the owner to bring water samples in, too."

"Good. Never hurts to have a water sample on hand. It could be something in the feed. Did he say anything about that?"

"He's pretty insistent that the alfalfa is good quality," I said. "I didn't see any ulcers on gross or anything suspicious in the stomach contents. I saved a large container of the stomach contents that I'll send over as soon as it clears for rabies. I don't think it's blister beetles if that's where you're headed."

"Yes, I was considering that. But sounds like a red herring. It could still be a toxic plant in the alfalfa, though, like yellow star thistle." She pursed her lips again. "What about the pelleted feed?"

"Yeah, I thought about that, like sulfur or a mycotoxin or something. I'm not sure about the brand or the quality. I asked him to bring a sample in."

"Glad you did that." Sandy nodded slightly. "Do you know if it's a new bag?"

"I didn't ask," I said, shaking my head. "I told him to stop feeding it, though, and save the bags."

"Good thinking," she said. "Have Anna send back the water and feed when the owner brings it in. We can do a visual inspection right away."

She chewed on the tip of her reading glasses, thoughtful.

"I'm thinking we test the feed for sulfur as a start. What do you think?" I asked.

"That's easy enough. Just put the request in." She shrugged, not convinced. It was a cheap enough test that could be done relatively quickly. It didn't hurt to run it to be safe.

"How'd the liver look?" Sandy asked.

Picking up what she was putting down, I answered, "The liver looked and felt normal. I thought about pyrrolizidine alkaloids or aflatoxin or something. I guess it could still be...." I shrugged. "But I'll have to wait for histo to make sure the liver has no significant lesions."

I was hesitant to ask the next question, but dove in anyway. "The owner keeps mentioning a pissed-off ranch hand and thinks the horses were poisoned. Thoughts?"

Sandy leaned back again and pursed her lips. "Not sure about that. I don't know why people are always quick to blame someone else for their bad fortune. Even if it was malicious, there are a million ways someone could've killed those horses. Cyanide comes to mind. Rat bait is less likely since there was no bleeding on necropsy. I think we need histo first."

"I was thinking the same thing," I agreed.

"Monensin would be on the list, too," she added.

"Oh! I didn't think of that. The cattle are out on pasture, and the horses are in stalls, but it's easy enough to mix feed bags if they're kept together. I'll ask him."

Monensin was a common feed additive for cattle that was lethal to horses. Ranchers were usually educated on that nowadays, and mix-ups didn't happen often anymore. However, I couldn't rule out feed-swapping yet, whether accidental or purposeful.

"Circling back to a toxic plant theory," Sandy said. "There's a laundry list of possibilities. Did Charlie have a look at the alfalfa bales or walk the farm?"

If a pasture wasn't managed properly, toxic plants could get accidentally baled in the alfalfa. And, if the person feeding the horses didn't know any better, contaminated bales could kill several horses. I thought it was less likely, given that Adam said he'd used the same person for his feed for several years. But the weather had been unpredictable, and weird plants were springing up. Further, they might have had somebody new driving the baling tractor.

"No, I don't think Charlie walked the farm or checked the feed. I think he only looked over the other horses. Are you thinking of a field trip?" I smiled, feeling a tickle of excitement. I loved going on farm visits with Sandy.

"Yes, ma'am," she said, smiling back. "I wanna see that alfalfa for myself, pick a few bales apart."

"I can ask the owner. What day is best for you to go out there?"

Sandy put her glasses back on and peeked through an old-school paper calendar she had on her desk. The days were splattered in almost illegible scratches in different colors of ink. With running the lab, teaching at the veterinary school, and leading continuing education for veterinarians, she was a busy person.

"The earliest I can go is Wednesday. Does that work?" She peered at me over the rims of her reading glasses.

"I'll check and get back to you. Thanks, Sandy. I'll keep you posted."

"Happy to help any time. I'll let you know if I think of anything else." Sandy turned back to her computer, sliding her reading glasses back up her nose.

Even though I'd hoped Sandy would come to the rescue with a slam dunk, I was secretly grateful that I wasn't the only one completely befuddled by this case.

* * *

I was closing Sandy's door when I noticed Gerald coming down the hall. My heart sank; a run-in with this troll was the last thing I needed today.

"There's the little lady," he said, his voice syrupy and patronizing.

I fought the proverbial vomit in the back of my throat.

When I first started at the lab, I'd politely asked him to stop calling me "lady" or "girl" and commenting on my looks. Instead of being cool about it, the turd-bucket started doing it more often, getting off on messing with me.

"Hello, Gerald," I said, trying to be polite and hating myself for it.

"Thought I'd look in on my favorite pretty face and give you a verbal on the steer from yesterday." He shifted his body, blocking me against the wall without touching me.

I cleared my throat, and his gaze lifted from my chest.

"My lab isolated *Mannheimia* out of the lung already. Bacterial pneumonia, just like I said. I'm always surprised about how often my lab provides hard evidence to confirm your guesses."

I clamped my fists so I wouldn't smack him. Gerald had perfected the art of being condescending and misogynistic while couching it in half-baked compliments.

"Thanks for the update," I said as I squeezed past him, feeling him leer at me as I fled to the receiving department.

Anna was busy at the computer, entering the information from the afternoon drop-off. She looked up as I approached with a smirk on her face.

"Gerald is such a prick," she said sympathetically, having heard every word of the short exchange in the hallway.

I smiled at the show of female solidarity. Until the lab director decided to do something about it, we'd all just have to suck it up. All of the women in the lab hated him, and some had even complained to Fran. But because he hadn't laid a hand on anyone, the boss was happy to look the other way. Gerald was just trying to be nice, she'd say. We all knew that was a load of dog shit. The guy might be good at his job, but that didn't excuse the perpetual harassment.

"Has the guy who brought the horse in this morning come back with the feed and water yet?" I asked.

"No, ma'am," Anna said.

"'Kay. I'll leave the paperwork here and remind him if we don't get it by Monday morning."

I reached over for a submittal form and started filling it out. I checked the boxes for a sulfur test and visual inspection of the pelleted feed. If anything else needed to be done based on what she found, I trusted Sandy to add it on.

"When he comes in, can you send the samples back to the toxicology lab?" I asked.

"Yeppers," Anna said as she took the paperwork.

She added a sticky note saying that the samples would be dropped off later. With thanks and a wave, I headed back to my office. Though I had just gotten off the phone with Shadowhawk's owner less than an hour ago, I needed to get that field trip set up. With lead in my stomach, I dialed Adam's number.

"Hello, Adam here," he answered.

"Hello, Mr. Williams. This is Dr. Harjo again." Before he could ask, I added, "I don't have any updates for you just yet. But I talked to Dr. Bishop, the toxicologist, and I have a few more questions for you."

"Okay," he drew the reply out hesitantly.

"Do you feed the cattle any pelleted feed?"

"No, ma'am. The cattle are on pasture. They get salt licks. That's it."

"Okay. Thank you. I just wanted to make sure the horses didn't have any access to monensin."

He huffed. I couldn't tell if he was laughing at me, frustrated, or something else altogether. This guy was a hard read.

"Dr. Bishop and I would like to come by and do a farm visit to look for toxic plants or other poisons. It'll also give us a chance to inspect the alfalfa. Would that be okay with you?"

There was a beat of silence on the other end of the line, and my skin prickled with an unsettling feeling. Usually, people were more than happy to get any kind of help they could, especially when they were losing animals. That pause was a ginormous red flag.

"Mr. Williams? Did I lose you?"

"I'm here," he said stiffly. "That'd be fine. When did y'all want to come out?"

"Would Wednesday be okay?"

"Is it really gonna take that long to find an answer?" he asked, frustration and anxiety ringing in his voice.

"I hope not," I answered, feeling my stomach clench. "But this is an unusual case. I want to get it on the calendar."

Adam harrumphed. "I'll make Wednesday work. What time?"

"How about nine? I'll see if Dr. Anderson can join us," I offered.

"Is this gonna cost me anything?"

I wasn't surprised by the question. Typically, animals didn't have health insurance. Vet visits and testing at the diagnostic lab could get pretty pricey. Even if the animal was highly valuable, like the horses at JW Ranch, a couple of thousand dollars was quite a bit of money.

"Your tax dollars will cover me and Dr. Bishop, being from a state lab and all. Dr. Anderson may charge, though."

I knew it wasn't fair to ask the vet to come for free. Most rural vets didn't make squat and often heavily discounted their services for the struggling ranchers. But vets had bills, too; most of them had some of the highest student loan debt across all professions. Some even lived below the poverty line. That was one of the reasons why veterinarians had the highest rate of suicide. The pressure of debt on one side often warred with their desire to help animals in need. Snarky owners who didn't understand the costs only made it worse. Some owners were downright cruel and abusive to the veterinarians who were trying to help their pets.

"I'll make sure he lets you know if he's coming and what the charge will be if he does," I continued. "You'll get to approve any charges before he comes out."

"Okay," he grunted.

"I'll give you a call as soon as I have more information. See you Wednesday."

After polite but stiff goodbyes, I picked the phone back up to ring the vet. Dr. Anderson was out doing pregnancy checks, so I left a message with his receptionist about the planned visit to the ranch.

By the time I had wrapped everything up, I was grateful to see that the workday was just about over. The Shadowhawk case was nagging at me, and I felt discombobulated. I was looking forward to the distraction of cooking dinner; Laila was coming over tonight and would help me shake the heebie-jeebies.

CHAPTER
SIX

I was surprised to feel intense relief when I pulled into the sanctuary of my driveway. I hadn't realized how much the Shadowhawk case was niggling at me.

Yersi greeted me at the door, meowing. He wove in and out of my legs as I set my stuff down. This time, I had the grace to keep the tower of books on the entryway table in their semi-precarious position.

"Yes, yes. I know," I said, unable to keep the smile from my voice. It felt good to be needed.

Merf, Yersi replied.

He sat down by his food bowl, tail swishing. He was practically pointing at the bowl and then his mouth, like in *Simon's Cat*. I tipped half a can of wet food into his bowl before starting dinner for Laila and myself.

After running my eyes over the fridge, I sighed, grabbing the lonely, moldy loaf of bread and tossing it in the trash. I hated wasting food, but I didn't want to die from mycotoxins produced by the mold on my bread, either.

Cooking was my thing, and I was pretty damn good at it. But I actually had to have food in my fridge to work my magic. I liked to go all-out when I had company over, but the plans with Laila had been a bit last-minute, so I hadn't had any time to shop. It was Friday, and I was running low on just about everything. I wracked my brain on what to make. Thankfully, I had a box of garbanzo-bean, spiral pasta in the cabinet; I could build off that.

Grabbing a basket, I headed out to the garden. The heat of the early summer evening settled around me, the sound of the cicadas filling the air. I ran my fingers through the sage near my back door, releasing the smell into the garden.

I loved my place for a lot of reasons, one of them being that it was *mine*, the first place I'd ever lived in that wasn't a rental. We'd been dirt-poor growing up. My dad had dipped before I was born and just left my mom and me in the dust. Though I was happy to see that shitass in the rearview mirror, only having one income was a struggle, and we'd jumped between rental slums. Mom had done her best; I'd always had food and clothes. And she'd made sure I went to school and got good grades. But she'd never owned a home.

I'd been a bit nervous about buying a house when I was already shackled with some pretty hefty student loan debt. I'd scrimped and saved for a down payment. When this place came on the market, I couldn't resist the cute one-bedroom and bought it about three years ago. It had been built back in the 1930s, but the age of the home gave it more charm. Situated in a quiet neighborhood, my place was within walking distance of the library, the art center, and a few restaurants. It also sat on a quarter acre of rich, bright red Oklahoma soil, the perfect land for creating a garden getaway.

I weaved through the garden and picked fresh basil. I added a zucchini to the basket; it was a great way to sweeten a pesto sauce. Sheltered from the hot summer sun was a bed of lettuce that was still growing strong. I harvested a couple of varieties for a mixed salad. I grabbed two handfuls of bright red cherry tomatoes, a lemon from the tree, and eggs from the coop. The girls had done right by me, and now, I had enough eggs to make dessert.

The garden was my favorite thing about my home. When I'd first moved in, I'd torn out the water-guzzling scraggly lawn, turning the space into a lush oasis. A mix of fruit trees and flowering bushes formed a semi-circle around a circular patio. Comfy chairs and a table sat beneath a latticed pergola covered with grapevines. The right side of the yard was dedicated to a series of raised beds for veggies and herbs. An Eglu with four chickens was tucked on the left side of the yard. They were softly clucking, starting to get settled for the evening.

With the pot of water set to boil on the stove, I made a quick pesto sauce with toasted garlic, walnuts, cooked zucchini, olive oil, a spritz of lemon, and basil. I also whipped up a quick batch of almond butter cookies for dessert. They were my one weakness, and I'd gotten the cooking time down to twenty minutes, including the time in the oven.

As I poured the cooked pasta into the strainer, Laila knocked and let herself in. Just hearing her knock put a smile on my face, and I felt my shoulders relax. She brought joy wherever she went.

Laila was petite, with brown skin and straight, jet-black hair that came to her shoulders. After moving from India to complete her Ph.D. at OSU, she'd decided to stay on as a now-tenured professor in the plant biology department. She was extremely smart and enjoyed life with every fiber of her being. I loved her dearly and appreciated her persistent, positive energy.

It was lonely in both our professions. Laila and I had both moved around a bunch for our education, making friends and then having to leave them behind as we moved to the next leg of our journey. I had lots of friends, just none of them in Stillwater. It was also hard meeting local people in a post-COVID world. Being an avid tabletop gamer, I'd tried a couple of Meetup groups. Unfortunately, I never really clicked with any of them. I was super grateful for Laila and didn't know what I'd do without her.

After a quick hug, she followed me into the kitchen and sat at the island. Yersi jumped up onto the stool next to her, purring as she gave him scratches.

"The usual to drink?" I asked.

She nodded as she leaned back to let Yersi settle into her lap. "Thanks."

As I set a glass of sweet tea in front of her, I asked, "How're things?"

"Pretty good. Been super busy. How 'bout you?"

I shrugged one shoulder. "Today was rough. Had a crappy case that's gonna hang over me all weekend. Kinda sucks, especially after the awful date yesterday."

"What kinda case was it?"

Though Laila didn't like the smell of dead animals or the sight of blood, she loved the mystery of the cases that came across the necropsy floor. I shared the details of the Shadowhawk case with her. Her eyes grew wide at the mortality rate.

"What do you think it is?" she asked, intrigued.

I shook my head. "No clue right now. Could be viral. Could be toxic. I won't know until I can get more testing done. I just worry going into the weekend with no answers. I don't want any more horses to die."

Laila smiled sympathetically. "That's what makes you good at what you do. You care. It's an interesting case, though. Do you think someone poisoned the horses?"

"It's unlikely. A lot of owners think someone offed their animal, but that rarely happens. Could be an accidental poisoning, I guess." I chewed on my lip.

"What happens if it was malicious?"

I sighed. "Animals are technically property in the state of Oklahoma. But we do have animal cruelty laws. Legally, all I have to do is issue the final report to whomever submitted the case. But, if someone poisoned these horses, I'll probably call the SPCA at a minimum. The horses are insured, so there will be a whole cascade effect from that, as well."

It always frustrated me that animals could be abused and killed, and there wasn't much the authorities could or would do about it. Unless they could tie it to a larger crime, like abuse of a person or if the animal was a police dog, it usually wasn't worth the paperwork. Most offenders walked away without prison time, even with a conviction.

Laila, sensing that I was slumping back into depression, reached over and squeezed my arm. "You'll figure it out. You're smart as hell.

Plus, it's probably something like a trace mineral in the water or low magnesium in the feed or whatever."

I flashed her a smile of thanks as I dumped the cooked pasta in a serving bowl and tossed it with the pesto sauce.

"Sooo…how about the date? What happened?" she asked, then raised both her hands in defense after seeing my face. "Never mind if you don't want to talk about it."

"Oh, lord. It was so awful, Laila." I laughed.

Laila leaned forward in her chair, elbows on the counter, eager to get the deets. "Did you honestly go on a date smelling like a dead animal?" she teased.

Huffing a little, I said, "It's what I do. Sometimes, I get a stinker."

"He was so sexy in his pics, though. What happened?"

As we took everything to the table and sat down, I shared the story in excruciating detail. When I got to the part about the attempted kiss, Laila cringed.

"That's rough. I'm sorry."

"Yeah…I think I'm done with the whole dating app thing." I sighed.

"What! He was literally your first Match date," she said, her eyes wide.

"It's like impossible to meet anyone our age," I huffed, feeling sorry for myself. "When everyone was chasing each other in college, I was busy getting my degrees. Now, all the good ones are snatched up. It isn't worth the time."

"Well, you don't have to date unless you want to. But, if you do, you'll find someone. You just gotta keep looking." She flashed me a hopeful smile. "And, when you do, they won't mind the smell of dead animals."

We laughed and dug into our food. As per usual, Laila had brought me out of my swirl of worry; I felt relaxed and happy again.

"How's work been for you?" I asked.

"Meh." Laila shrugged. "We got that big grant I was telling you about."

"That's great news!" Then, I crinkled my brow, unsure why getting money to continue her research was *meh*-worthy.

Laila noticed and said, "I know. The grant's the good part."

I made a "keep going" gesture with my hand.

"Okay, okay," Laila shifted in her seat. "It's just that the Department Chair position is opening up soon. I don't want Ian to get it. I'm not sure I can stand working for that guy."

"How's that related to the grant?" I asked, completely confused.

"Well, Ian and I went for the same grant, and I got it. He's already gunning for me after that. And…." She fidgeted with her fork. "I just don't want to work for him if he becomes Chair."

Ian was a fellow plant biologist in her department. His specialty was growing climate-change-resilient corn, and he was in direct competition for the same grants as Laila. He was also a total racist and treated Laila with constant disdain. I was betting he was supremely pissed about her getting the grant and would probably target her for the next few months.

"Screw that guy." I waved dismissively. "You should go for Chair. You'd be a rockstar."

Laila's cheeks flushed with embarrassment, and a small smile danced on her lips. "I've been thinking about it, actually. A couple of faculty members have come by, offering support if I do go for it. I don't think they want Ian as a boss either."

"It's not just about picking anyone but him," I said, trying to reassure her. "People like you. Plus, instead of competing against everyone, you help them, like as a mentor and stuff."

Most academicians were like sharks and hardly any had a single altruistic bone in their body. It was all about competition: getting the most grants, publishing the most papers, and stepping on the most people to get to the top. It was an eat-or-be-eaten world. Academia was just like corporate America, but they hid the back-biting under tweed and elbow patches.

Laila was one in a million and stood out in the sea of tweed. Bucking the system, she went above and beyond to help others. She often provided feedback on grant applications, assisted with publications, shared teaching material, and passed on grant leads with other faculty. Some academicians hired three grad students on the same project, with the winner taking all. In contrast, Laila would pick the right project for the right student, setting them up for success and making sure they came out the other end with the Ph.D. they deserved. She was a keeper.

"Seriously, I think you should go for it," I nudged. "I'd like to have you as a boss. Better than Fran, for sure!"

Laila looked down at her plate, still poking the pasta. "Yeah, I don't know why she lets Gerald treat you and all the other women like that. She's just as bad as him by turning a blind eye. Same with Ian. Someone has to speak up about men like them and help change that behavior."

"I've tried," I said, frustrated. "But without support from higher up, things have just gotten worse."

Laila shook her head. "It's gotten to the point where women just tolerate it because there isn't much else we can do if we want to keep our jobs. It sucks."

I nodded. I also felt helpless.

Laila waved her hand to brush the negative thoughts away and took a bite of pasta before saying, "Anyway, we'll see about the whole Chair thing. How about you? Any cool cases lately?"

"Oh! You're gonna love this one." I couldn't help but snicker as I remembered the story from earlier in the week. "A student comes in with a bottle of lotion. She said she found an animal part in it and showed it to her teacher, who confirmed it was a mouse femur."

"Like a teacher at OSU?"

"I don't know. I'd be desperately worried about our education system if it was." I laughed. "Anyway, she pulls out this fancy lotion bottle and a plastic baggy with a chunk of lotion-covered funk."

"Ugh…I'm still eating!" Laila gagged.

"You asked." I shrugged as we shared a smile. "So, I took a look at it for free, and I can tell right away it's just old lotion gunk. You know, the kind that builds up around the lid?"

Laila nodded, digging into her salad.

"I am trying to explain to this chick that it's most definitely *not* a mouse part," I continued. "She insisted it is and wanted to sue the lotion company. I offered to do histology and cultures to confirm, which she said she wanted."

"Who would pay for that?" Laila asked, eyebrows raised.

I smirked and shook my head. "I know, right? It ended up costing her like two hundred bucks. I think she was convinced she was gonna make major moola off this. Anyway, I do histo, and it's just a huge mat of fungus. They cultured *Aspergillus* out of it. Of course, no animal parts."

"Oh, my god. That is so disgusting." Laila grimaced.

"After I issued the report, she came by again. She insisted that her teacher said it was an animal part and that I didn't know what I was talking about. I tried to explain to her that having large mats of fungus growing in your fancy lotion is the *exact* reason why beauty products have a shelf life. She was pissed. She insisted on having everything back to get it tested somewhere else."

"Good luck with that," Laila snarked. "She should've used that money to buy a fresh bottle of lotion!"

"Exactly!"

Laila shook her head. "I don't know how you deal with all of those wackadoodles."

"Yeah, sometimes, I wish we had a buffer, like human medical pathologists have with the cops," I replied. "I don't mind the grief counseling part of it. But when someone is shouting at me that a mat of fungus in her lotion is a mouse femur…yeeeah…not so much fun."

"See, that's why I work with plants." Laila smirked. "There are no crazy owners. And I don't come home smelling like a dead animal."

"To each their own. I'm not sure I could spend my days reviewing data on water consumption rates, growth rates, and the sizes of millet seeds on your mutated babies," I teased.

Laila dramatically raised her eyebrows, opened her mouth, placed her hand over her heart, and fluttered her eyes, feigning shock. "You dare call my babies mutated?"

"Well, they are."

We both laughed.

"Anyway, that fungal mat was just the start of my week. Today majorly sucked. Glad you reached out. I needed my weekly dose of Laila."

The conversation shifted to lighter topics as we finished dinner, bussed the dishes into the kitchen, and loaded the dishwasher. Though we were both tired, we decided on a quick game of Carcassonne.

As we munched on cookies and laid out the game pieces, Laila asked, "What're you up to this weekend?"

She drew a castle piece and claimed it.

"Netflix," I answered. "I'm on-call."

I drew a crappy road and decided to place my meeple on a farming slot. It was a risk locking in a meeple so early in the game, but I figured I already had one completed castle in that location and could expand if Laila didn't block me out.

"Want to be my backup at a department party?" she asked. "I know it'll be a bunch of stuffy plant biologists. But it'll get you out of the house, and the food is usually pretty good. It's to welcome a new prof from Romania who's doing his sabbatical here. How about it? If you get a call, you can flake and not worry about it."

She countered my farming with a well-placed cloister with a triple road.

I shrugged. "Sure, why not? When is it?"

I added another road piece that headed away from where I was planning to build my empire.

"Sunday evening. I know you usually have brunch with your aunty, but it starts at six. You'll have plenty of time to chillax in between. I'll pick you up at five thirty?"

Her next piece was a castle, and she had no choice but to add to my farmland.

"Sounds good," I said.

We continued laying down pieces, and the conversation shifted to lighter topics. I ended up winning, but it was close. The risk I'd taken by farming early had paid off. I'd even been able to block her from stealing it. I'd take the win; I needed it today.

At the end of the game, we decided to call it a night. It had been a long day for both of us, and we were tired. At the door, she gave me a long hug.

Sensing the weight of the day on my shoulders, she said, "Don't worry, sweety. You'll figure that case out. You always do. *And* you'll find someone who loves *all* of you…even if you come home smelling like ass."

She gave me a wink as she headed out.

CHAPTER
SEVEN

Sunday morning, I woke up to Yersi making biscuits up and down my back. I had tossed and turned all night and was reluctant to leave my cozy bed. But Yersi was having none of that. I shifted so that he would roll off next to me.

"Ugh, Yersi. Stop already," I grumbled, pulling the covers up to my chin.

Merf, he answered.

He started rubbing against my head purring. The little bugger was so cute, I had no choice but to give him scratches before I climbed out of bed.

I shuffled into the kitchen in my slippers and started the kettle. Yersi swirled around my legs, meowing. The kettle kicked off just as I finished dropping half a can of cat food into his bowl. After setting my tea to steep, I checked my phone.

There was always an unshakable, low level of anxiety when I was on call. Even though all my patients were dead, there was always the risk of an outbreak, and I couldn't just stuff a carcass in the fridge until Monday. The phone felt like a leash sometimes. Having the Shadowhawk case hanging over my weekend didn't help things.

To my relief, I didn't have any notifications. No work calls also meant that another horse hadn't come in from JW Ranch since Friday. I was hopeful it would stay that way.

I piddled about the house and the garden, enjoying my quiet time, feeding the chickens, weeding, and watering. The girls were excited to be out of their enclosure for a few hours and were enthusiastically scratching around the yard, clucking softly to each other.

It was a beautiful Oklahoma morning, and the garden was busy with wildlife. Bees bobbed along the flowers. Hummingbirds zipped and chirped at each other, fighting over the feeder hanging from the pergola. The resident squirrel watched me from the safety of the grapefruit tree, tail whipping up and down, barking at me. The soft sounds of my girls rustling about the yard and the sweet smell of jasmine helped me relax.

With the raised beds watered, I had about an hour before I needed to leave for brunch at Aunty's. Grabbing a book, I decided to read outside in the cool morning air. Yersi hopped into the other seat, languidly stretching out, tail swishing as he watched the birds in the trees.

Yersi was only allowed outside under very strict conditions. First, he had to stay on the back patio. Second, he could only be outside when I was with him. Finally, if he so much as tensed when wildlife was out and about, it was back inside lickety-split for the troublemaker. Surprisingly, he did a pretty good job of obeying the rules. I guess he thought being a great slayer of canned food was enough for him to feel macho.

Some people gave me crap for keeping him as an indoor-only cat. If the threat of being hit by a car or eaten by a great-horned owl weren't enough to deter those nay-sayers, I'd remind them that house cats kill an average of 2.4 billion—yeah, billion with a "b"—birds a year in the U.S. That usually shuts them up.

Yersi turned to look at me, eyes squinting in the sun as if he knew I was thinking about him.

Yeah, you. You little bugger.

His tail started swishing, and he closed his eyes languidly.

I cracked open *FKA USA* and started reading. The sunlight trickled through the leaf cover, dancing across my skin as a soft wind blew through the trees. I was soon lost in the story.

After a bit, the soft alarm on my phone signaled that it was time to head out to Aunty's. I quickly shooed Yersi into the house, and he obliged, even if it was at a meandering sashay. I tossed on a comfy cotton dress and left my hair loose. Grabbing the stack of books to return to Aunty, I headed out for brunch.

Between dinner with Laila and the quiet time in the yard, I could finally put the debacle of Thursday's date behind me. The experience was slowly turning from a humiliating moment in my dating career to a great bar story. I was sure my vet school friends and I would laugh ourselves to tears at the next conference.

I still couldn't fully relax, though, and I realized that the Shadowhawk case was still floating around at the edges of my mind as mile after mile passed on my way to Aunty's. I turned the music louder, trying to chase the bad thoughts away. Deep down, I knew I wouldn't be able to fully put that case aside until it was solved.

* * *

Every Sunday, I made the two-hour drive to see my Aunty Molly in Ada. She was my anchor, and I treasured each meal with her. The visit would be a much-needed respite after a rough week. The tires crunched on the gravel as I rolled into Aunty's driveway just a few minutes before 11 A.M.

The chickens were out scratching in the front yard, undisturbed by my appearance. Aunty had a fairly large flock, much bigger than mine. She had a mix of Rhode Island Reds and Plymouth Rocks, which she kept for their eggs. Over the years, she'd built what was affectionately known as Chicken Alcatraz. It was a nearly impenetrable structure that kept the birds safe. If Aunty was home and Chula was outside, she'd let the girls out to forage in the verdant garden. Otherwise, they were kept in lockdown.

Sure enough, Chula was on guard when I pulled in, lounging on the porch, watching the chickens. Seeing the car, she came barreling down the steps, tail wagging.

Chula was a medium-sized, brown mutt with one ear that flopped over and one that stood up straight. She had a lean body, a semi-thick coat, and a bushy tail. Aunty swore she was half-coyote. I honestly didn't know what was in her genetic soup and was too cheap to do one of those dog DNA tests. At the end of the day, all that mattered was that Chula was sweet and took care of Aunty.

"Hello, Chula." I bent down to massage her soft, velvety ears. "Come on, girl." I patted my leg, and she followed me up the rickety front steps.

Aunty's house was over one hundred years old and sat on three acres. The wood-plank siding on the tiny ranch-style had been sanded and repainted a cheery yellow with white trim about four years ago. A large wrap-around porch boasted wicker chairs with plush cushions. Potted plants filled the space and blended into the traditional medicinal plants that were arranged along the border of the porch. I took a deep breath, inhaling the sweet smell of the jasmine that was climbing along the porch beams.

I loved Aunty's place and had spent many hours on the porch, watching the chickens scratch in the yard and listening to the singing of cicadas. If the wind was just right, the soothing smell of lavender would drift over from the adjacent farm. It was the best spot to watch sunsets. I loved my place, but Aunty's house was a second home.

Aunty's front door was open, but the screen was closed to keep the flies out. I rapped on the metal door lightly and let myself in. I held the screen for Chula, who trotted in after me, tail still wagging. She snuffled around the skirt of my dress, smelling the black Yersi hair that seemed to cling to everything I wore.

Aunty was at the stove, cooking French toast. Seeing me come in, she grinned from ear to ear and bundled me into a floury hug. Aunty was short and heavy-set with light brown skin. She wore her sixty-plus years proudly, with her hair almost entirely gray and pulled back into a long braid.

"Are these new?" I said, touching her earrings. "The beading is beautiful." I noticed she was wearing a matching bracelet.

"Aren't they lovely? Casey made them. Oh!" She held up a finger before heading back to her room and returning with a small box. "I got these for you."

I opened the box. Inside was a lovely pair of beaded earrings. Concentric diamonds in blue and purple formed the top of the earring. Dangling below were several beaded lines with drop shapes on the end. I couldn't tell if they were peacock feathers or tears.

"Aunty! I love them." I grabbed a pen from my purse to hold my hair back in a bun and put the earrings on. "How do they look?"

Aunty smiled, eyes shining with pride. It was all the answer I needed.

She gave me another hug and then went back to cooking. I grabbed a knife and started cleaning the strawberries. Chula's toenails clicked across the floor as she sniffed around for anything that might have been dropped.

"How's work?" she asked.

"Meh." I shrugged.

"Meh?" She put her hand on her hip, spatula still in hand, as the first piece of toast cooked on the cast iron pan.

"Yeah, meh. I had a tough case on Friday, and it's been eating at me. I can't stop thinking about it."

She lifted an eyebrow and motioned for more details before flipping the toast over.

"Several horses are dying on a ranch north of Stillwater. Just stressed since I don't know what's causing it."

I didn't go into more detail about the case. Aunty was super smart and worked at the Chickasaw Nation tribal library. She was well-read and could talk for hours about the history of the first peoples. She also loved nature, knew her medicinal plants, and could hold her own when talking about ecosystems and environmental protections. That being said, her eyes always glazed over with boredom when I geeked out on her in vet-speak, so I spared her.

"I know those types of cases mess with your head. Just remember to take care of this…." She tapped over my heart with one finger. "So that this is free to work the problem." She motioned to my head. "Trust that the answer will come."

I knew she was right. I needed to let the worry I held in my heart go so my mind would be free to work the case. It was just damn hard to separate myself from the threat that still hung over the ranch. I didn't want any more horses to die because of me.

She gave me a half hug before she flipped the first cooked slice of French toast on a plate and dipped another one. I finished cleaning the strawberries and popped one in my mouth before I sat down.

"What would you like to drink?" she asked.

"Tea, please. Want me to make it?"

"I got it," she answered, waving me off kindly. "I know what will help."

A few minutes later, Aunty set down a steaming cup of homemade honey lavender tea before returning to the stove to finish the last few slices of French toast. I took a deep breath of the sweet lavender smell and closed my eyes. I felt my shoulders relax. I thought I needed caffeine, but Aunty was right. The herbal tea cleared my head as my heart released the anxiety.

"How's the library?" I asked.

"Pretty good. They finally got the air conditioner fixed."

She set the finished food out on the table, and we dug in.

"Finally!"

"Right? Halfway through the summer, but…." She shrugged without finishing the sentence. "There are some books for you by the door. Don't forget them on the way out. Read *A Snake Falls to Earth* first. You'll like that one."

Aunty always made sure I had plenty to read, checking out books and sending me home with a new stack every weekend. She was trying, somewhat unsuccessfully, to pull me out of sci-fi and into another genre.

"I just finished *The Kaiju Preservation Society,*" I said. "I've got it in my car with some others to return. Don't let me forget to give them back to you before I go."

"Did you like it?" she asked.

"It was fun. I liked Jamie's snark."

Aunty smiled, pleased. She loved finding books for people to enjoy.

"I'm about halfway through *FKA USA*," I continued. "It's pretty hilarious. I needed the fluff—thanks for recommending that one."

"Did you try *Gone Girl*?" she asked.

I nodded hesitantly. "I tried it. It's just not my thing. I get enough of that stuff at work."

"Fair enough," she said, unperturbed.

We chatted a bit more about her work and books before she asked, "What else have you been up to? Didn't you have a date this week?"

"Oh, god, don't even ask." I rolled my eyes.

"That bad?"

"That bad," I confirmed. "It was like going on a date with Zuckerberg."

Aunty burst out laughing and waved her hand dismissively. "Harjo women don't need a man anyway."

I shook my head, smiling; I knew she was right. I didn't *need* a man. But it would be nice to have a partner to share dinners with, a travel buddy, and someone to come home to on crappy days like Friday.

With the last slice of toast cooked to perfection, Aunty laid out the food on the table. I grabbed three slices, drenched them in real maple syrup, and dug in. As Aunty's meal hit my stomach, the last little bit of anxiety slipped away.

"Thank you, Aunty. I needed this."

We casually finished off all of the food on the table, minus a few bites snuck to Chula under the table. With the dishes cleared, Aunty nursed a cup of herbal tea as I washed up.

"What are your plans for the rest of the day?" she asked.

"Laila invited me to a faculty dinner tonight."

"In the plant biology department?" she asked, eyebrow raised. "Blech."

"Yep," I answered, smiling.

She shook her head. "That sounds like torture."

I laughed and then shrugged. "It probably will be. But it's Laila."

Aunty nodded. She knew Laila was a keeper and understood why I'd want to take one for the team.

"You probably don't have time for a walk, then?" she asked.

After stuffing ourselves on brunch, Aunty and I would usually sit on the porch and watch the chickens as we digested for a bit. Then, we'd often go on a walk along the creek. Aunty loved to point out the plants and animals. We'd also bring bags to pick up any litter that we would find. We were both pretty big on doing our part to keep our world clean.

I shook my head, slightly disappointed that we would be cutting the usual routine a bit short. "I should probably head out soon. I need to get back and change before she picks me up. Sorry I couldn't stay longer," I said with genuine disappointment.

"Next weekend, then," she said, smiling.

"It's a date." I flashed her a smile back.

After everything was all cleaned up, Aunty walked me to my car with Chula following close behind. She folded me into a hug. I dug around in the backseat and traded the books I had in my car for the new ones she had checked out for me.

"Remember." She tapped over my heart. "Take care of this."

I hugged her again.

Filled to the brim with love and fully recentered, I climbed into my Prius and pulled out of the driveway with a wave.

CHAPTER
EIGHT

I made it back home in the midafternoon, still stuffed from brunch, with plenty of time to get changed for Laila's shindig. I sat on my bed, staring at my closet, unsure of how fancy the dinner was going to be. At a loss, I grabbed my phone to text Laila:

Whats the attire for tonight?

Just wear a casual dress or something

I smirked. I should've known she'd answer like that. Laila lived by the seat of her pants. She often didn't worry what people thought about how she looked or what she wore. Laila had a charisma of twenty, though. She could get away with that; I couldn't. I still needed to dress appropriately for the event to be able to surf the political seas successfully.

Trying to tease more details out of her, I texted:

What r u wearing?

Haven't decided yet

I rolled my eyes. It was like pulling teeth.

Can't blame me for what I pick then

Just don't smell like dead animal

She added a kissy-face emoji, and I couldn't help but let out a low laugh.

Turning back to my closet, I decided on a short-sleeve, dark blue dress. It was a fit-and-flare style that accentuated my curves but had a loose enough waist that I wouldn't be uncomfortable all night. To my delight, the new earrings from Aunty matched the embroidery on the hem perfectly. I left my hair loose and wavy and skipped makeup.

When I heard Laila pull up outside, I slipped on a pair of navy flats and grabbed my purse.

She leaned over and opened the door for me.

"Your outfit is perfect, as usual," she said, smiling.

"With no help from you!" I teased and flashed her a smile back.

Laila was dressed in business casual, with a deep purple blouse paired with fitted dress pants. I'd guessed the event attire perfectly.

"Thanks again for coming with me," she added. "The visiting prof is nice. But Ian's gonna be there. So...." She shrugged, knowing I would fill in the blanks.

"I got you," I said as I piled into the car.

* * *

About thirty minutes later, we were knee-deep in the political quagmire of the plant biology department, clutching our drinks.

The event room at the Atherton was surprisingly packed. Oklahoma State was an agricultural school, but I hadn't realized how large the plant biology department was until today. I'd wandered the halls of the Physical Sciences Building and been out in the test fields, but I'd never been to one of their functions. The noise of a dozen excited conversations filled the space as a gaggle of faculty members, graduate students, and the occasional bored partner mingled.

Laila introduced me to several people whom I immediately forgot.

I had the hardest time with names, no matter how interesting people were. I smiled politely, and my thoughts drifted as they talked about plant-gene-this or USDA-grant-that. They smiled politely back when I shared what I did at the veterinary school. The Chair position came up more than once, and I was delighted to hear that Laila had garnered strong support from most of the people in the room.

The drinks flowed freely, and within an hour, a few attendees were already slurring their words. It didn't help that we were all coasting on semi-empty stomachs. Instead of a sit-down meal, "dinner" turned out to be various canapés, which was a fancy way of saying that we only got a few Ritz crackers with cheese. I had to eat about twenty small plates of various bits and bobs to satiate my growling stomach. Sticking to fizzy water also helped keep my head clear.

As I made another raid on the canapé table, I noticed a weasel-like man swoop in on Laila. Her shoulders immediately tensed, and I could tell she loathed this person despite the smile on her face. Based on her response, I could only assume this was the infamous Ian Murray. I'd heard my fair share about this little shitass, but I'd never met him in person.

I made my way over to her, back straight, to offer my support.

The man towering over Laila was about six feet tall, extremely thin, pale, and had a narrow, pinched face. His hair was thick and immaculately groomed but clearly dyed to cover the gray. Deep furrows lined his forehead, and permanent frown marks drooped on either side of his weak mouth. He wore a stiff, button-up shirt and slacks with pointy dress shoes.

As he shifted his piercing vulpine gaze to me, he asked, "And who is this?"

The hair rose on the back of my neck. I suddenly felt like I was in the woods at night being hunted by the big bad wolf.

Trying to hide my apprehension under a thin veneer of confidence, I said, "Dr. Josie Harjo. I work in the vet school. I'm a friend of Dr. Yadav's."

His grip was limp and sweaty as we shook. "Dr. Ian Murray. You've probably heard of me."

"Oh, yes. Your reputation precedes you," I answered sweetly.

A flash of a smirk crossed Laila's face before she caught herself.

Missing the exchange, Ian gave a self-satisfied smile and said, "Then I am sure you're aware that my lab is the largest in the department. Corn is an important staple of the American diet. Unlike some of the lesser grains, like millet."

Laila stiffened. We'd both caught the dig.

"Because of solid funding, my lab supports three graduate students and has some of the most advanced equipment for genetics research," he boasted.

I tried not to roll my eyes. I knew exactly what his lab did, and the sequencing equipment hadn't changed much in the last twenty years. The bullshit was strong with this one.

"I even have a patent pending," he preened.

Laila coughed lightly to cover up what I was sure was going to be a laugh. Anyone who publicly bragged about their grants, publications, or patents most likely sucked at their job. The real winners kept their noses to the grind to get 'er done. I knew for a fact that Laila had more than a handful of patents, but she was humble about it. Though I was trying to keep my smile cooly polite, I could feel it turning sour.

His eyes drifted down to my chest, and he offered, "I can give you a tour of my lab sometime."

Good lord, there's no end to it.

I had to bite back the proverbial vomit in my throat.

"No, thank you," I said, trying to keep my smile polite while adding to myself, *No fucking way, creep.* I was sick of indulging this twerp.

His eyes glided up to my face and narrowed, taking in my darker skin tone before landing on my earrings. A slight sneer twisted his lips.

"Are you native?" he asked.

I was still mentally trying to wipe off his lascivious gaze, and his comment caught me off guard. My eyebrows shot up, and my shoulders tensed.

"Excuse me?" I asked, certain that I'd heard him wrong.

"Yes, you must be," he said with certainty. His shoulders shifted, and his eyes drifted from me to Laila and back again. "Aren't you girls cute? An Indian with a dot and an Indian with a feather."

I felt a rush of adrenaline and almost slapped him. My cheeks grew warm with fury.

"Ian," Laila practically growled. Her polite smile had dropped, and anger filled every muscle in her face. I knew her well enough to catch the flash of rage and the quick clench of her hands. "That comment was inappropriate. Please behave professionally," she said in an icy tone.

Ian's shark eyes caught hers, and he smiled smugly as if he sensed blood in the water.

"You are so emotional, Dr. Yadav. You know I was just joking. You need to relax." He took a sip of his drink, and his eyes flashed like a vampire. "I've heard that you're seeking support for the Chair position." He let out a low, patronizing laugh and tapped the nail of his pointer finger on his glass. "Sweety, you should leave that to the big boys. Someone so sensitive isn't suited for leadership. Emotional women make great mothers. You should consider having children before it's too late. You're getting a bit old."

Before I could jump in to defend her, Laila's eyes narrowed, and I sensed that the lioness was about to attack. I grabbed my imaginary bag of popcorn and sat back to watch. This shitass deserved what was coming.

"I prefer growing millet, Dr. Murray. The farmers appreciate my millet genes, especially with the drought and all. I'll focus on passing those genes on for a while since they keep my lab fully funded." Though her tone was matter-of-fact, subtle derision laced her words.

Ian's back stiffened with the jab.

He opened his mouth to respond, but Laila cut him off. "And, yes, I *am* applying for the Chair position. It's important to have a strong leader in that role. One who is willing to support her colleagues instead of stabbing them in the back."

His lips tightened into a straight line just as mine started to turn up into a smile.

Before he could respond, Laila grabbed my elbow and gestured across the room to a man standing alone by the drink table. "Oh, look, Dr. Varoujan appears to be free. Let me go introduce you to our guest of honor, Josie."

"It's been a pleasure," I said with syrupy fakeness. I wanted to make sure he knew exactly how I felt about him.

Laila nodded to Ian stiffly before we both glided away.

Laila leaned over and whispered in my ear, "Sorry about that. You'll like Armand. He's one of the good ones."

Dr. Varoujan looked up at us as we approached and threw Laila a welcoming smile. He reached out to shake her hand.

"Nice to see you again, Dr. Yadav. Rumor has it that you helped arrange tonight. Thank you." His voice was deep, and he had a slight Eastern European accent.

Dr. Varoujan stood a couple of inches taller than me, with almond skin and dark, wavy hair that tickled his ears. He was broad-shouldered but not imposing, with a slim waist and muscular legs that pulled slightly on his khakis. His eyes were a deep brown with smile creases at the edges.

I felt a tingle of instant attraction.

"I'm glad you could join us for the next three months," she answered before turning to me. "Dr. Armand Varoujan, this is Dr. Josie Harjo."

His handshake was firmly confident but didn't crush my fingers. I noticed his hands were slightly calloused and then blushed at the thoughts that came after.

Laila caught my response and covered up a conspiratorial smile.

"Nice to meet you. So, you're here on sabbatical?" I stuttered out, trying to regain my composure. Thankfully, I could still string a sentence together.

What the hell? I'm acting like I'm fifteen! I took a deep breath.

He kindly pretended not to notice my embarrassment. "Yes, I work at the Agricultural Sciences University in Romania. We're trying to identify strains of drought-tolerant wheat. I'm hoping to spend some time in Dr. Yadav's lab this coming week."

"We're excited to have you," Laila said.

"And, you? What's your area of research?" he asked, looking at me with genuine curiosity.

"I'm a veterinarian, actually. I work over in the diagnostic lab."

"Really? How did you get suckered into a party with stuffy plant biologists?" he asked with a half-smile. His posture was relaxed and welcoming.

"Laila." I nodded my head towards her, and she grinned.

"She must be a really good friend. Or she's blackmailing you," he teased.

"Why can't it be both?" I joked back.

He laughed as Laila playfully slapped my arm.

"Josie is like a coroner for animals. She spends most of her day knee-deep in horse guts." Laila said and then casually popped a canapé in her mouth.

My heart sank. This was the part of the conversation when guys typically got grossed out and politely excused themselves.

Then, he surprised me by saying, "Interesting. What's that like?"

"It's kinda cool, actually," I answered cautiously. "Every day is a new puzzle to solve. Keeps me on my toes."

"I see Jan flagging me. I'll be back," Laila interrupted, dropping me a quick wink before she left.

After Laila disappeared, Armand gestured to a seating area near the drink table. "Would you like to sit?"

"Yes, thank you."

He led the way, trailing a faint, pleasant smell of aftershave. We grabbed two cushioned chairs facing each other. He set his drink on the table between us. Leaning forward slightly, he rested one elbow on the armrest and laced his fingers. I sat back, trying to appear relaxed, and sipped my drink.

"A veterinary pathologist," he said, eyes excited. "That's fascinating. What's the weirdest animal that you've autopsied?"

"It's called a necropsy in veterinary medicine," I corrected and then kicked myself. It was my auto-response, and I'd blurted it before I could zip my lips. "It's a common mistake," I added, hoping I hadn't offended him.

Armand rolled with it, unphased. "Huh! I wonder why they use different words," he mused with genuine curiosity.

"I have no idea why it's called a necropsy when it's on a non-human," I said with honesty. "I'd have to Google it. Maybe it has to do with word roots? Like 'auto' means 'self' and 'opsy' means 'to examine? So, if a person is doing a medical examination on a person, it's 'autopsy,' but if it's a person examining another animal, then it's 'necro' for 'dead thing' in general…so 'necropsy'?" I caught myself rambling and took another sip, trying not to geek out too much on him.

"Huh." He flashed his eyebrows up and nodded.

"To answer your question," I continued, "the weirdest thing I've ever necropsied is a giant millipede."

"A giant millipede?" he exclaimed, incredulous. "Why would anyone want a necropsy on a giant millipede?!"

I smiled. "It was a subspecies of giant millipede that's endangered. It was part of a zoo collection's breeding program. Why are you all judgy about bugs?" I teased. "They do necropsies on bees and stuff, too. Insects are important."

He held up his hands. "I know, I know. Believe me, being someone who researches crop health, I understand the importance of the ecosystem. I just didn't know they did necropsies on millipedes."

"I am pretty sure that all AZA-accredited zoos and aquariums have to have necropsies on any animals that die in human care. But I'm not sure. I don't do exotics very often. It's mostly dogs, cats, horses, and cows where I work."

"So, what did you find? How did it die?" he asked.

"Sadly, it had sat under the heat lamps for some time before the keeper found it. It was mush by the time I dissected it. I threw some special stains on it. All I could say was that I didn't see any fungus or mycobacterial organisms."

"Huh," he said again. "How often are you able to determine the cause of death?"

"Most times, we get an answer. Sometimes, the animals are too rotten, though, like the millipede. Sometimes, there are lesions, but all of the testing comes up negative, and I can't say for certain the exact cause. Rarely, we don't find anything at all. But I would say ninety percent of the time, we get an answer one way or another."

"Have you had any interesting cases recently?" he asked.

My stomach clenched, thinking of the Shadowhawk case. Happy that he was showing genuine interest in my work, I didn't want to ruin the conversation with that black cloud. Instead, I shared the parvovirus case I had this week and then talked about how common the disease was in the state because of the puppy mills. He seemed genuinely interested, and I relaxed into my nerd-speak.

"What led you to veterinary pathology?" he asked.

"I used to read Patricia Cornwell books when I was little."

"The Kay Scarpetta books?" he blurted, surprised.

My eyebrows shot up. "Yeah. Have you read them?" I asked, slightly shocked.

He nodded. "A few. A long time ago. I haven't read them in a while, but I remember just enough to be dangerous." He flashed a playful grin.

I laughed. "I wanted to be a coroner like her. But, during undergrad, I got a job on the necropsy floor at the vet school and fell in love with veterinary pathology. In human medicine, autopsies are all just gunshot wounds and heart attacks. The veterinary pathology world is like a buffet of death. I get to work with a gagillion different species with a myriad of diseases. In Oklahoma, we see a ton of infectious diseases and toxicities, which I love. It's super interesting. Plus, unlike Scarpetta, I don't have to go to court as a veterinary pathologist…. Well, at least I haven't had to go yet."

I took a sip of my drink, watching him over my glass. He appeared unphased by my talk of death, but I'd only scratched the surface of what I do. He hadn't *smelled* it yet.

"I like those investigative stories. I've read the *Hot Zone* a couple of times," he added.

"That's a good one. I've read it a couple of times, too. That book got me into viruses and infectious diseases. Did you know Nancy Jaxx was a veterinary pathologist?"

"Really?!" he asked, flabbergasted.

"Yup. There are a ton of veterinarians who work for the Army and the government in general. Vets lead most of the food outbreak investigations, too."

"Huh! I didn't know that." Holding up his thumb and pointer finger about an inch apart, he said, "I was about this close to going into the medical field. I find pathology fascinating. But I decided on plant biology instead."

"What made you change your mind?"

"I decided to help people by trying to make sure they have enough food. I remember the food lines when I was little, and I don't want people to go through that again. Granted, it was politics that created the breadlines back then. But, with climate change, we're going to start seeing it again if we don't act quickly. We need to find more sustainable wheat varieties that can be grown in harsh conditions." He shrugged. "That's what I'm hoping to do. Help people by making sure they have enough to eat."

I nodded with a smile. It was a worthy cause. "It's great that your university allowed a sabbatical. That's a thing of the past nowadays in the U.S. We're lucky to get even a week off for continuing education."

"Between the war and the drought, the wheat yields have dropped almost in half. We supply a lot of grain to the Middle East and Northern Africa. We need to get production back up, or we will be facing famine in those regions. The university sees that. So, we received some extra funding to travel and share ideas with other researchers. I'm looking forward to working with Dr. Yadav. She's done some great work that might translate to other grains."

"Yes, Laila's a keeper for sure." I smiled with pride.

The conversation flowed naturally from there. Not only was he intelligent, but he was easy to talk to and seemed genuinely interested in the world around him. I started to feel bad that I was monopolizing his time, but he seemed comfortable and didn't appear eager to mingle with others. A few faculty members wandered over to introduce themselves, but they would eventually drift away, and I'd get him all to myself again. It wasn't until the clock hit 9 P.M. that I looked up and realized that most of the attendees had left.

"Hello, you two. Have a nice time?" Laila asked.

"Yes, we did. Thank you for introducing us," Armand said as he stood. He turned to me with a soft, welcoming expression. "I'd love to see you again for lunch or something."

"Sure, that sounds great. Here." I handed him my phone to enter his number and then texted him so he'd have mine.

And, as if sensing something good in the room that needed to be shat on, Ian joined us.

"There's Count Dracula," Ian said. "I see you've enthralled our little vet friend."

I couldn't stop myself from huffing audibly. Apparently, Ian was a bigot to women *and* men.

Armand was unfazed. Ignoring Ian, he reached out to shake Laila's hand. "Thanks again for the wonderful evening."

He then turned to me and took my hand gently. "I'm really glad we met. Look forward to seeing you again."

Another straggler swooped in to say their goodbyes to Armand, and Laila and I took the opportunity to escape.

Back at home and relaxed from a nice day with Aunty, Laila, and Armand, I kicked my shoes off and checked my phone. I hadn't gotten any calls from work, which was a win. And I had a text from Armand waiting for me. Double win.

> It was great meeting you. Are you free to grab lunch this week?

> Nice meeting you too. How about Thursday?

Within a few seconds, he thumbs-upped my text.

> Noon work? Where do you want to go?

> Have you been to Red Rock?

> No but happy to try it

I thumbs-upped his text and sent him the maps link.

It wasn't until I was tucked into bed with a purring Yersi that the dread of the Shadowhawk case settled back over my heart. I'd have to face reality tomorrow, and I'm pretty sure it was waiting for me with a bat.

CHAPTER
NINE

The voicemail light was blinking ominously when I entered the office Monday morning, and I felt a tightening in my stomach. It was pretty rare to get any phone calls on the office line. If anyone had questions about a case, they'd email me. I apprehensively picked up the phone, keyed in the password, and listened.

"Dr. Harjo, this is Adam from JW Ranch." His voice was shaky over the noisy large machinery in the background. "We found another horse dead this morning. Please call me as soon as you get in." He left his phone number before the voicemail ended.

I rubbed my forehead, trying to keep myself together. Even though there was nothing I could have done differently, the weight of the new death hung over my shoulders.

With a deep breath, I dialed Adam's number, and he answered immediately. This time, there was no background noise.

"Hello, Adam here."

"Mr. Williams. This is Dr. Harjo. I just received your message." I paused, fumbling for the best way to say my condolences. "I'm sorry for your loss. Is now an okay time to talk?" I leaned over my desk, cradling the phone.

"Yeah." His voice was resigned but much less shaky.

"What can you tell me about the recent death?" I asked gently.

"Last night, my wife and I checked on the horses. They all looked fine. Then, this morning, I found Twilight Messenger dead in her stall."

"I am so sorry." My brow furrowed. "Was she eating and drinking normally?"

"Yes, ma'am," he replied curtly.

"Did she leave her stall at all? To go out to the arena or anything?"

"No. We didn't take her out all weekend."

"What did the bedding look like in the stall?"

"Pardon?" he asked, not understanding the question.

"I mean, was there any blood, signs of thrashing, was the feces normal? That kinda stuff."

I tried to stick to open-ended questions. Those often led to the most truthful answers. But I didn't have a choice with this one.

"The bedding was all messed up, if that's what you mean. Didn't see no blood. Why? You think she was murdered?" His voice was anxious and gruff.

"I don't know what happened." Trying to calm him down, I added, "I'm just trying to gather as much information as possible right now."

Given the tousled stall bedding and the information from the other dead horses, I was fairly certain the horse had either been in extreme pain or had been seizing before it died. Whatever was happening on the farm, I'd bet dollars to donuts it was causing neurological disease. It could still be viral, but I was leaning more toward a toxin. And the horses had to be getting a pretty big dose to have the mortality rate this high; it certainly had the feel of intentional poisoning.

"Anything else out of the ordinary this morning? Do any of the other horses look ill?" I asked, trying not to lead him with the questions.

"No, ma'am."

"Do you have a camera system in the barn?" I asked, certain there had to be more to the story. Some of the classier ranches did have cameras in the barns, especially if the horses were valuable. They were also part of a wider security system, including fire alarms.

"Yes, ma'am. Should I check the video?" he asked, doubt creeping into his voice.

My eyebrows crinkled. Wouldn't that be the first thing someone would do if they had a camera in the barn?

"Absolutely. And, if you see anything unusual, please let me know ASAP," I nudged, trying to get him to understand the importance. "Save the video, too. If it's all right with you, we can watch it when we come by on Wednesday. Do you have any video from when the other horses passed?"

"No. The system rewrites every twenty-four hours."

My heart sank a little, and I kicked myself for not thinking of this earlier.

"That's okay," I responded. "Would you like to bring Twilight Messenger in for necropsy? I can't guarantee an answer, but it will improve our chances of solving this quickly."

"We already buried her with the tractor this morning. I think my wife would kill me if we dug her back up."

Perplexed, I frowned slightly. My pen twirled back and forth between my fingers, tapping on my desk, an annoying nervous habitat I couldn't shake. It made sense that a rancher wouldn't want to leave dead animals lying around, but the horse had been buried pretty damn fast. The more animals we necropsied, the better our chance of figuring out what was happening at JW Ranch. I was surprised he didn't wait to bury the horse until he talked to me or Charlie first. I was certain Charlie would have advised that he bring the horse in. There were now twelve horses left on that farm that could die at any moment.

"I'm hoping we can figure out what's happening before another horse dies," I said, "but if not, it's really important that you bring any other animals in. The more information we have, the better the chances are that we can save the rest of your horses. And, if you notice any horses walking funny or looking off, call Dr. Anderson right away."

I was met with silence that stretched awkwardly between us. I'd seen my fair share of odd ducks in this line of work, but Adam was quickly moving up the top ten list.

"Did you bring the water and feed by yet?" I asked, trying to get the call back on track. "I haven't had a chance to check with the receiving department."

"Yes, ma'am. Left it in the drop box," he said irritably.

"Thank you. I'll make sure it gets back to the toxicology lab as soon as we hang up."

"When are we gonna get an answer?" he pressed.

I felt my hackles go up. I took a deep breath, trying to stay professional.

"We have to make sure it isn't rabies before we can do any other testing. I'm hoping to have more information for you this week. But I can't promise anything. I'll call you as soon as the results come out." I felt my attempts at reassurance bouncing off him like a brick wall.

He said his thanks in a tone that implied it was more out of polite habit than a genuine appreciation. The guy was a tough read, and I couldn't tell if he was angry, frustrated, or both. I also couldn't completely rule out that he was being cagey for another reason.

After hanging up the phone, I leaned back in the chair. This case was messing with my head. I felt awful for Adam, but something was off about this case. I had a nagging feeling that I was missing something.

* * *

Eager to put this case to bed, I headed to the toxicology lab. Dr. Bishop's lab was one of the largest in the country and boasted all of the bells and whistles. Her team could perform most of the toxicology testing in-house, and only a handful of tests were send-outs. Given the number of toxicities and accidental poisonings in Oklahoma, it was a nice resource to have on-site.

When I walked in, the two techs were busy at the benches, dressed in lab coats, gloves, and eye protection.

"'Morning," I called out, putting my lab coat on and grabbing a pair of gloves. "Did you all get the overnight samples yet?"

"They're still in the basket," one of the techs said, pointing to the bench in the front.

I dug through the basket of samples until I came across the feed and water from JW Ranch. Pulling the samples and paperwork out, I spread everything out on the table. I wasn't a toxicologist, but I wanted to see everything with my own eyes.

I picked the jar of water up first. There was no evidence of cloudiness or discoloration. I popped the lid and took a whiff. Everything checked out okay, which was what I expected from functional stall waterers drawing from a city line. But several toxins could hide in clear water that didn't have a smell. The toxicology team would have to take it from here. I put the lid on the jar and set it back down.

The pelleted feed was still in the original bag, which was about a quarter full and rolled shut. With a gloved hand, I sifted through the feed and pulled some out to have a closer look. It was a mixture of small, light brown pellets and rolled corn. There was no obvious mold, but several of the pellets looked swollen, like they had been exposed to water. I rolled a bit between my fingers, and some of the pellets crumbled instantly. I couldn't smell anything other than the dry, grassy scent of feed. I rolled the bag back up and returned it to the basket.

"Hey, y'all. Can you please STAT these samples and give Dr. Bishop a heads up when she comes in? Several horses have died already, and it's pretty serious."

"Sure." One of the technicians came over, grabbed the samples, and started reading through the paperwork. "Dr. Bishop has a continuing education event until lunch, but we'll let her know."

Trusting the lab to have my back, I thanked them and headed back to my office. I checked through my pending box to see if any results had come back. The microbiology results from the steer were in, and, as Gerald had already informed me on Friday, they'd cultured *Mannheimia* spp. The virology was also back, and the lung had tested positive for Bovine Viral Diarrhea Virus. It was a classic case of bovine respiratory disease. The owner was lucky they got an answer with the steer being so rotten. The ranch would have a tough time trying to manage the BVD, though; that virus was difficult to eradicate from a herd.

The viral results were back from the puppy, too. As expected, the intestine was positive for parvovirus, and I wouldn't have to look at anything under the microscope for that case, either.

It felt good to have a couple of cases buttoned up. It felt even better when I could knock a case out without doing histology, getting an answer and saving the client some money. But the satisfaction of those two cases was dampened by the thought of the horses at JW Ranch. I desperately wished I'd get a slam dunk on the Shadowhawk case soon.

* * *

Trying to shake off the gloom, I went out to the necropsy floor to check if anything had come in overnight. Sure enough, there was a cat from the teaching hospital laid out on the table. I threw on a lab coat and shoe covers before heading out onto the necropsy floor.

Dustin was already out there, setting things up when I made my way out. "Hey, Good Lookin'" was pouring from the radio, and Dustin was merrily singing along.

"Morning, Dustin. How was your weekend?"

He turned the music down before answering. "Pretty low-key. Went fishing. You?"

"Yeah, it was nice. Distracted me from this." I waved my hand around the necropsy room. "Remember that neuro horse from Friday?"

"Yep."

"Another horse died over the weekend."

He grimaced in sympathy. "They gonna bring it in?"

"Nope. They already buried it."

Dustin looked at me, surprised. "Really?"

"Yeah. Kinda weird, right?"

"Were they worried about the cost of doing another necropsy?"

"I don't think so. Since the horses are insured, you'd think they'd want the necropsy. I wonder if they only brought that other horse in because Dr. Anderson told them to." I shook my head. "Are the rabies results back yet?"

He looked at me incredulously, one eyebrow arched. "Seriously? It's Monday morning, and we're talking about the state lab here."

We both laughed. We were the only publicly funded lab in the state that worked weekends, and I should've known better.

"If we're lucky, we may have something this afternoon. But I wouldn't hold your breath," he said.

I grabbed the paperwork for the cat and read through it. Many animals coming over from the veterinary school hospital came with answers. This one was no exception.

Sometimes students would ask why the faculty bothered to order necropsies when they already knew what was making the patient sick or why it died. I tried to impress on them that there was a lot to learn about a disease by looking at patients who had been affected by it. Each body was a gift and provided more data that could help other patients in the future.

The patient before me today was a seventeen-year-old, female, domestic short-haired cat. She'd been diagnosed with intestinal lymphoma three years prior. There'd been an initial response to chemotherapy, but three months ago, the patient had re-presented with signs of diarrhea, lethargy, and weight loss. Ultrasound and fine-needle aspirate confirmed the involvement of the liver and spleen. Despite another round of chemo, the cat had rapidly declined. The owners had elected humane euthanasia and were kind enough to consent to necropsy.

Though the patient had come with a diagnosis of cancer, the results of the necropsy would help the oncologists better understand disease progression, extent of organ involvement, and degree of response to therapy. This, in turn, might help improve therapeutic protocols for future patients.

Eager to lose myself in an easy case, I looped my hair around a pen and snapped my gloves on.

"I put out a scalpel because it's a cosmetic necropsy. Do you want your knife instead?" Dustin asked over the music.

"Scalpel is perfect, thanks."

A cosmetic necropsy essentially meant that the body had to look pretty when we were done. Owners usually requested this service when they wanted the body back for burial rather than group or private cremation. Because of that, we had to collect samples from both body cavities through a small incision in the abdomen. A scalpel blade was perfect for the delicate dissection a cosmetic necropsy required.

After removing the abdominal organs, it was obvious that the poor cat had been riddled with cancer. The intestine was diffusely thickened, with almost no lumen on cut-section. The liver and spleen were diffusely pale and soft. All of the lymph nodes were enlarged. There were even white nodules in the kidneys. The cancer had spread everywhere within the abdomen.

I collected samples for histology, knowing the oncologists would want information regarding the microscopic appearance of the neoplastic lymphocytes. Though it always made me sad to know the cat had been so sick, I was glad we could get information to help future patients.

The organs from the thoracic cavity looked clean on gross examination. The lungs were soft, fluffy, and floated in formalin. The heart was a normal size, shape, and color. I'd still run histology on the thoracic organs, as microscopic metastasis was possible.

Despite the limitations of the cosmetic necropsy, I could still collect most of the samples I needed from the internal organs. I skipped collecting bone marrow because I'd have to crack a femur to collect it, and it was hard to pretty that up when I was finished.

I also passed on collecting the brain. The cat hadn't been neurologic, and it would have been a major pain trying to get that out and putting everything back together after. I'd done a cosmetic necropsy on a neurologic rat before; that wasn't something I'd want to repeat on *any* species.

After all of the samples had been collected, we placed the organs in a baggie and put them back in the body. I then carefully stitched the hole closed, burying the sutures. Dustin and I spent extra care washing all of the blood off, trying to make the body look as peaceful as possible. I never knew if the owners would have a peek in the bag or not, and I wanted to be respectful.

Within less than an hour, we had everything buttoned up and the table cleaned. I said my thanks to Dustin before tromping through the footbath and taking my protective gear off.

Back in my office, I was able to write the report and release it before lunch. It was a cut-and-dry case, which I appreciated. I hadn't realized how much I'd needed one of those to boost my ebbing confidence.

CHAPTER
TEN

Since there were no more carcasses waiting for me, I decided to escape from the looming trepidation over the Shadowhawk case and attend the Woman's Forum lunch on campus. I hoped it would be a nice diversion.

The Woman's Forum was held monthly with topics ranging from grant writing to networking. The talks were usually pretty good, and they always had food. I didn't know what the topic was today, but figured I'd head over. Ever since my college days, I couldn't pass on a free lunch.

I grabbed my water bottle and locked up my office. When I left through the front doors of the lab, a wall of heat and humidity enveloped me, and sweat instantly beaded on my skin. The familiar sound of cicadas filled the air.

Despite the oppressive heat, I enjoyed the short walk east to the heart of campus and Willard Hall. In my humble opinion, Oklahoma State was the most beautiful campus that I'd seen, and I'd been to several on the guest-lecturer circuit. Large brick buildings with white columns were sprawled between sweeps of immaculate lawns shaded by mature trees. The heat had chased students inside, but when the weather was less brutal, students were usually planted across the campus on benches and at outdoor tables.

I entered Willard Hall, back into the sanctuary of air-conditioning. I could hear the buzz of people talking from the hallway and made my way into the seminar room. A small stand in front listed today's topic: "Work-Life Balance: How to Have a Career and a Family."

I felt an instant wash of irritation and briefly thought about high-tailing it out of there. But I was already here, and free food was calling me. Feeling grumpy, I headed into the room.

The place was packed, and a long queue wove from the buffet along the edge of the wall. Several people were already seated and chatting over sandwiches. On the stage, a handful of women were getting settled behind the panel table. The host was micing up; a loud tapping sound filled the room as she tested it.

Still feeling annoyed, I joined the queue and looked around for someone I knew. To my relief, I spotted Laila walking from the front of the line, plate and drink in hand. I called out and waved to her. She made her way over.

"I didn't know you were coming this month," Laila said, smiling warmly. "I thought you were on duty this week."

"Yeah, I'm on duty. I lucked out, though. Just one case this morning, and it was easy. Figured I'd stop in." After I beat, I added somewhat rhetorically, "What's up with the topic today?" I shook my head in disappointment.

She looked at me, confused. "What do you mean?"

"I guess...." I paused, trying to find the right words. "Men don't have panels on how to balance work and a family. Why do women? That's bullshit."

Seeing the double standard, she snorted softly in agreement. It made me feel better that I wasn't the only one who didn't like the chafing straight-jacket that society had cinched around women.

Having identified the source of my angst and vented it to my BFF, I tried to let it go and appreciate that the women on campus were even willing to support each other. Aunty's generation wasn't so fortunate.

She'd always been told that only rich, white women went to college, and, even then, it was only to find a husband.

I looked down at Laila's plate and drink. "Want to grab a seat, and I'll meet you?"

"Sure. I'll save you a spot." She flashed me a smile before weaving through the tables and claiming a space.

The lunch was kinda *meh* today. But I didn't look a gift horse in the mouth. I selected a vegetarian sandwich, took an extra helping of potato salad, and skipped the cookies. I settled in next to Laila with my plate and water bottle.

"How are things with you? Have you put in your application for Chair yet?" I asked, digging into the potato salad.

"I did." Laila smiled conspiratorially and leaned over. "And…put feelers out for support. I think I might even get it!"

"That's awesome! Congrats! You'll totally get it." I shoveled another bite of potato salad into my mouth.

Potato salad was one of those things that just about everyone could make, and it would taste okay, but very few people could make it taste *great*. This potato salad was delicious with just the right amount of mayo and pickle. I suspected it came from campus catering, who, despite all of the crap people talked about them, could make one mean potato salad.

Laila smiled, and I couldn't tell if it was at my comment about the position or at me snarfing down the food.

"Well, I honestly don't want the gig." Laila took a bite of her sandwich and continued around a mouthful of food. "I've got enough on my plate. But I can't let that douchebag get it. And I think a lot of other people don't want him to get it, either. Thanks for coming last night. If you can believe it, that's him behaving himself."

I rolled my eyes. "He's such a shitass. That behavior is gonna kill his career."

She waved her hand dismissively. "I've lost patience with him." Then, her mouth stretched into a mischievous grin. "Speaking of last night…you and Armand were quite the pair."

"He's pretty cool." I looked down, feeling shy, and smiled. "Thanks for introducing us."

Her eyebrows shot up, and she bumped me with her elbow. "And?"

I felt a stupid grin spread across my face. "We're having lunch on Thursday."

"Ohhh! That is awesome! I knew you'd like him." She took a self-satisfied bite of her sandwich.

"Because I like wheat genetics?" I teased.

"Because you both have the same sense of humor. And you both like plants. And he's single. *And*…I'm pretty sure he'd be okay if you showed up smelling like a dead animal." Laila flashed another big smile.

I couldn't help myself and burst out laughing. A few people in the audience looked over. But since the talk hadn't started yet, I didn't feel bad.

"He seems genuinely interested in what I do. It's kinda refreshing," I conceded.

Laila nodded smugly.

The lights dimmed, and the host stepped up to introduce the panel. The panel included a physics professor, the associate dean of the veterinary school, an English graduate student, and a drama professor. During the first half of the session, the microphone was passed to each panelist as they shared their journey and how they balanced a successful career and a family.

I was pleasantly surprised to hear that they had selected panelists with a breadth of experiences and perspectives. Some had kids early in their academic careers, while others waited until they were firmly settled in a faculty position. The number of children they had and their ages spanned a wide spectrum. Their life-partner situations also varied, from never married to divorced to long-term partnerships. Some pregnancies were planned, and others were not. I appreciated the panelists' honesty.

The panelists did have one thing in common: They all gave the impression that it was damn hard to juggle work and a family, especially if they didn't have a solid support network.

The best piece of advice came from the drama professor, who recommended drawing strict lines between work and personal life, whether that personal life held kids or not. Otherwise, one aspect had the potential to heavily dominate the other.

After the last panelist spoke and the applause subsided, the host moved on to Q&A. A few underwhelming questions were asked and answered. Toward the end, a young woman raised her hand. The mic was passed to her, and she asked, "What if you have to choose between getting your PhD and having a kid?"

The associate dean of the vet school eagerly waved for the mic on the stage. The host passed it to her, and the associate dean leaned forward.

"There's a priority to things," she said resolutely. "First is God, then your husband, and then your family." With each item on her list, she pounded her pointer finger on her knee to emphasize her point, her flashy bracelets clanking.

Intending a mic drop, she dramatically leaned back and passed the mic back to the flustered host. With the associate dean's answer, the room fell deathly silent, and the other panelists shifted uncomfortably. The drama professor coughed and raised her hand. The grateful host passed the mic to her and stepped back.

"Everyone has their individual priorities." The drama professor leaned forward, trying to catch the young woman's eye in the audience. "Only you know what is important to you at each moment in your life. And those priorities may change."

The drama professor shifted and gestured to the other panelists on the stage. "Each of us has a different set of wishes and dreams. And our journeys are unique. For example, I did both—I had a kid in grad school. Others might have a kid before or after grad school. And others may choose not to have a child at all. There is no right or wrong answer."

She turned to make eye contact with the young woman again. "I know that's not the answer you are looking for. Both grad school and having a child are major life decisions. You, and your partner, if this is a shared journey, will need to weigh the pluses and minuses of both choices. And no matter how much you plan, life will still throw a wrench in the works. So, the best piece of advice I have to offer is to hang on and enjoy the ride. Many of the most unexpected adventures will be the best ones."

As the professor handed the mic back to the host, there was light applause around the room. The young woman smiled slightly and nodded her thanks.

* * *

After the panel was over, Laila walked me back to the lab with the early afternoon heat settling around us.

As soon as we were far enough away from the crowd, I blurted, "What was up with that comment from the associate dean?"

"I know, right?" Laila shook her head. "I'm pretty sure we aren't the only ones in the audience who don't believe in the Christian God."

"Right? And she assumes all women have a husband, or even a male partner for that matter." I *tsked*. "Then, she says husbands are more important than anything else."

"Well, except for God," Laila snarked.

I laughed sadly and then shook my head. "That might be how she sees things. And that's cool and all, but she's a role model to all of the women out in that audience. And she basically said, 'Do it my way, or you suck.'"

"She was definitely pushing a very narrow view." Laila frowned.

"It kills me when women in power proselytize a 1950s view of the world," I sighed, unable to hide the disappointment in my voice.

"What do you mean?"

"I mean…actions like hers undermine our experience. We need to show solidarity, not parrot the antiquated message of subservience to a husband or perpetuate religious bias."

"And assume everyone is straight," Laila added.

"Exactly! I just can't believe people still do that shit. It's like she ignores the part of her religion that says, 'love thy neighbor.' Sheesh." I waved a dismissive hand. "What a waste of an hour."

"At least the potato salad was good." Laila shrugged. "And kudos to that drama prof for speaking up."

I harrumphed, still irritated.

"I want to be like the drama prof when I grow up." Laila grinned. "She completely shifted the tone without publicly humiliating the associate dean. That was pretty damn slick. I wish I had those mad skills."

"Right? That was pretty badass." I looked over at her. "That's what's gonna make you such a great Chair: You care. You want to understand people and help them. We need more people like you." I gave her a half-hug.

She grinned ear-to-ear and threw an arm around my shoulders to hug me back.

"What's the rest of your day look like?" she asked.

"I'll have to see if any bodies are waiting for me," I sighed. "If not, I'll push some paperwork around and try not to stress over the neuro horse."

"Is that the case you were telling me about last Friday?"

"Yeah." I started chewing my cheek. "They found another one dead this morning."

"Oh, no!" Sympathetic worry creased her forehead.

"Yep. Pretty much sucks. I'm hoping to have the rabies results back soon so I can finally *do* something. Until then, my hands are tied."

"Well, I'll be sending positive vibes your way." She bumped me with her shoulder affectionately.

CHAPTER
ELEVEN

A refreshing wave of air conditioning washed over me when I entered the lab. I tried to shake off the grumps from lunch, but the associate dean's words still chafed. Before I went back to the office, I checked in with Dustin. He was at his desk in his coveralls, plugging supply orders into his computer, the familiar crooning of Hank Williams playing quietly in the background.

"Hey," I said, leaning through the open door. "Anything else come in?

He shook his head. "We got the rabies results back, though. Came back negative."

"Already?" My eyebrows shot up.

Dustin shrugged nonchalantly and leaned back in his chair. "Yes, ma'am. Kinda surprised myself. Got the call right before lunch. Must've done it when they first got in."

That was the quickest turnaround I'd ever seen from the state lab, and we'd been mocking them just this morning.

I felt my shoulders relax with relief. Hindsight was always twenty-twenty. If the horse had been positive for rabies, I would've had my ass chewed for being reckless. If the horse had been negative, and I'd waited all weekend to post it, I still would have had my ass chewed, especially with another horse reported dead this morning. I'd rolled the dice and lucked out this time.

"We should push the other samples out for testing today before it gets too late. Mind sending the frozen brain to virology for herpesvirus and West Nile testing?" I asked.

"Already done." He nodded slightly. "Walked it over as soon as I got the call from the state."

I couldn't help but smile. "Have I told you that you rock?"

"Nope." He shook his head and frowned with mock sadness.

"You rock," I said, grinning. "Did the brain make today's run?"

"Nah, but the virology lab said they'd run it tomorrow first thing. I tried to impart a sense of urgency when I dropped the sample off."

"Thanks for hustling it over there."

"No problem." He shrugged. "After hearing another one died, I figured all of the samples were STAT now."

I nodded, and after a beat, I said, "I'm gonna head out and sort through the rest of the stuff."

"I'll join you," he answered, following me out onto the necropsy floor.

With my lab coat on, I tied my hair up and snapped a pair of gloves on. Dustin pulled the Shadowhawk samples out of the fridge and laid them out. He was always on top of it, and I could hug him for it. I walked over to the counter and looked down at the pile of containers, chewing on my cheek.

"Whatcha thinking?" Dustin asked, curious.

"Just hard to know where to start," I answered.

Veterinary pathology was a whole different ball game compared to human pathology. In human medicine, pathologists could pretty much order whatever tests they wanted, and the county would cover the costs. In veterinary pathology, the owner often had to cover the costs out-of-pocket. If the animal had health insurance, it rarely covered post-mortem testing. Even if the animal had life insurance, the company would occasionally require a necropsy to pay out but wouldn't cover the cost of the necropsy itself. Despite our lab being heavily subsidized by the state, the lab testing could run thousands of dollars if I wasn't judicious. I was always balancing the owner's pocketbook with solving the case, which was an added layer of stress.

"Histology for sure," I said, talking through it out loud. "I need to get everything under the microscope. I'll start trimming as soon as we're done here."

I stared down at the rest of the samples spread out on the counter.

"EHV testing was the most important thing to get cracking on. Thanks again for that." I paused, looking at the frozen stomach contents, liver, and kidney. "It could be a toxicity or poisoning. But I think we have a better chance of finding something with the feed or the water."

Dustin grunted in agreement.

I took a step back from the counter and put my hands on my hips, still chewing on my cheek. Toxicology was a rabbit hole. If I didn't have a general idea of what I was looking for, I could easily blow five grand of the owner's money, throwing darts at a board with a blindfold on.

"Let's send the liver, kidney, aqueous humor, urine, and stomach contents to the toxicology lab to hold. Let's keep the CSF. I guess it could be equine protozoal myelitis, but the history doesn't fit. We'll just save it in case we need it."

"And the blood?" Dustin asked.

"Let's spin it and save the serum. Eastern and western equine encephalitis testing is a send-out to Texas A&M. I'll see what histology shows before we go that direction."

My gut twisted as I started adding up how much this would cost Mr. Williams. With the tests ordered so far, he was already pushing a grand. Instinct told me that I might be doing more toxicology testing, too. I kept reminding myself that these tests might save the lives of the other horses.

After packing everything up and thanking Dustin, I headed to the histology lab to trim the formalin-fixed tissues, swapping out my necropsy floor lab coat for my trimming one. I put my headphones in and turned on some hip-hop. It was the perfect trimming music.

Some pathologists would have the histology technicians trim all of their tissues, but I preferred to trim my own. The histo techs were awesome, and I trusted their skills, but if the histo techs trimmed the tissues, they would take one piece of each tissue sample in the bucket per SOP. Since I collected everything and the kitchen sink, they'd be dropping thirty-plus slides on my desk in a couple of days. If I trimmed it, I could pick and choose what I wanted, not having to worry about being buried in glass.

I put on new gloves and slid into one of the trimming hoods with the formalin jar for the Shadowhawk case. The small samples I'd collected on Friday would probably need to stay in formalin to fix for at least another day before they could be processed and ready to look at under the microscope.

Unfortunately, the organs that were of the most interest, the brain and spinal cord, would have to fix in formalin even longer, seven days or more, before I could try to trim them in. They were too mushy otherwise. Just the act of slicing them could cause artifact. If we weren't closer to an answer soon, I might have to shave a day or two off that fixation time, no matter the risk of damaging the tissue. There were lives at stake.

I drained the cloudy, brown formalin from the bucket, leaving a pile of partially fixed samples sitting in the sieve. With practiced ease, I worked my way through the tissues, making thin, nickel-wide sections of select organs with a scalpel and placing them into the histology cassettes. I'd done my fair share of crappy trimming jobs, tissue squishing through the waffle-like plastic of the cassette as the tissue expanded with further fixation. It only took a couple of poorly processed cases and side-eyes from the histology techs for me to learn the perfect size.

After snapping all of the cassettes closed, I loaded them into a processing rack with fresh formalin for further fixation. The technicians would run the processor overnight, and, if I was lucky, the slides would be waiting on my desk tomorrow afternoon. But the tissues were still a bit pink and didn't have the tan-tinge of fully fixed samples. The histo techs would check the sections before running the processor. If the tissues were still half-fixed, they'd hold the samples another day before putting them in.

I'd just have to wait for answers on this one.

* * *

It was mid-afternoon by the time I finished trimming. I decided to check in with Sandy before giving Mr. Williams a call about the rabies result. As I passed Gerald's office, his frame popped into the doorway and pounced on me.

"There's my little Pocahontas," he said with a slimy smile plastered on his face as he leaned against the door jam. "You're looking lovely today. Have you ever thought of being a model? You're very attractive even though your skin is a tad dark."

I bit back a snarky retort.

There were bigots everywhere; Ian Murray was a perfect example of this. But Gerald always knew how to get under my skin and had his own special way of torturing me. Trying to keep the moral high ground, I just raised my eyebrows and shook my head in disgust rather than hit him over the head with a two-by-four as I passed.

He laughed quietly behind me before turning back into his office.

I felt a surge of adrenaline. I clenched my fists and did my best to be kind and embrace the idea of live and let live. It was hard, though. Gerald was just downright evil, constantly pecking at people. No matter what I tried, he just kept at it.

Seething, I ducked into the toxicology lab. Sandy was in there, leaning against one of the lab benches in her lab coat, looking through paperwork.

When she noticed me, her eyebrows creased with concern, and she asked, "You okay?"

"Yeah, just Gerald being Gerald." I took a deep breath, fighting the effects of the adrenaline dump.

Sandy shook her head, frowning, and came over to hug me. "You know how tenured faculty are. They think they can crap all over everybody. And they're kinda right."

"Just because he's tenured doesn't mean it's okay to be racist or sexually harass people."

What can you do? Sandy's shrug said.

Sandy had the strength to roll right through the bigotry. Being a black woman in Oklahoma had been pretty damn rough, especially in a profession that had previously been dominated by white men. By keeping her head down and being downright awesome at what she did, she'd become the top veterinary toxicologist in the world.

That still doesn't make it right, I fumed. *People shouldn't treat each other like that.*

The ironic bit was that Gerald boasted about being a devout Christian. Yet, he completely missed the memo on treating people the way you wanted to be treated. I was equally pissed at my boss. Behavior like that was enabled by the higher-ups. Fran was also responsible. Just because Gerald was good at his job didn't mean that his inappropriate behavior should be excused.

The tech, Eva, who had been listening in, asked, "Want me to go kick his ass?" She said it with such a sweet, innocent smile and slow Oklahoma drawl that Sandy and I couldn't help but burst out laughing.

My tension eased a bit, knowing I was amongst friends.

"Nah, thanks for having my back, though." We fist-bumped, and Eva smiled back in solidarity. I thanked my lucky stars that everyone else I worked with in the lab was so damn cool.

Sandy waved me back to her office, where she cleared a pile of papers from the guest chair and circled behind her desk to claim her own. I was still a bit shaky from the altercation with Gerald, the last bit of adrenaline working its way through my system. I hated myself for letting him get to me.

Sandy leaned back in her chair, reading glasses hanging from a chain around her neck. Her hands loosely gripped the armrests. Her chair squeaked as she rocked slightly. She watched me closely, with worry creasing her eyebrows.

"Talk to me," Sandy prompted in a reassuring tone. "What's going on? Is it Gerald?"

I took a deep breath. "Gerald's a turd, but I'm used to it, sadly. He just happened to poke me on a bad day. This stuff with the Shad-owhawk case is wearing at me. They lost another one today."

Sandy whistled low.

"Yeah. That's four horses now. Please tell me you have something."

"You know I'd tell you if I did," she said sympathetically.

I nodded. Sandy was on her game. She cared about the animals and the customers. If she had anything, she'd make sure that information was shared as soon as possible.

"The water looks clean," Sandy continued. "Not too worried about that. We could look for blue-green algae, sulfur, and stuff like that, but my gut is telling me it's not the water. Lenny and I also sifted through the stomach contents. We didn't see any toxic plant bits or beetle parts. Doesn't completely rule that out, though."

"What about the feed?"

"I checked the brand and didn't get any hits for recent recalls. The sulfur levels were within the normal range. I think polioencephaloma-lacia is unlikely. I had a gander at the pellets. Some of them were swollen, like they'd gotten wet at some point, but there was no obvious mold. We could measure the aflatoxin and fumonisin concentrations in the feed."

Sandy lifted an eyebrow questioningly. Those were expensive send-out tests.

I chewed the inside of my cheek.

"I just sent the brain off for PCR for herpes and West Nile. I don't think it is viral, though. The horses are vaccinated, and the mortality rate is pretty darn high for that." I rubbed my forehead. "I just think it has to be some kind of toxin. But the access to toxic compounds is just so limited on the ranch. If it isn't in the food or the water, someone had to have brought a toxin into the barn."

"Are the horses insured?" she asked blandly.

My eyes snapped back to Sandy's.

"You think they're killing them for insurance money?" I asked, slightly aghast.

"Wouldn't be the first time," Sandy said, as if the words were salt in her mouth. "I had a rancher kill off his top red Holstein breeder for the one million in life insurance money. He poured weed killer on the feed. Took us damn near a month to figure that one out."

"The owner was acting a bit weird." I paused, thinking back to the interview and the subsequent phone calls. "He buried the first two, only bringing Shadowhawk in because the vet told him to. He'd already buried the one that died today by the time he called me. He was also a little nervous about us coming to the ranch on Wednesday. I still haven't figured out if the insurance requires a necropsy or a veterinarian's note to pay out."

"Worth looking into to cover your bases and all," she advised.

"Yeah, probably."

I'd done my fair share of reports for insurance companies. But, in those cases, the owners always wrote it on the form, knowing the insurance company would need a copy of the report directly from the lab for the payout. Until now, I hadn't fully realized how unusual it was that Mr. Williams *hadn't* written the insurance information on the form.

"Back to test options," I prompted. "I don't want to blow a ton of money chasing every single lead. But I don't want any more horses to die, either. I might not be able to wait until I get the histology back." I paused, chewing on my cheek again. It was getting raw. "I don't think it's aflatoxin. I've seen my fair share of that, and there was zero bleeding. I'm thinking we send the feed off for fumonisin. We can get a good look around at the ranch on Wednesday and suss out the owners some more. There's also this ranch hand that Mr. Williams keeps talking about. Then, we can see if we need to go looking for some of the less common things. What do you think?"

Sandy nodded. "I agree. Rule out the common stuff first. Hoofbeats and all."

"Thanks, Sandy. I appreciate you."

With a nod, I left her office to fill out the paperwork to send the feed out for fumonisin testing. Unfortunately, Anna said we'd missed the pickup for today, and the package wouldn't go out until tomorrow. It would take a week or more to get the results with the shipping time.

With a knot in my stomach, I knew that, once again, I'd just have to wait.

Back in my office, I called the main line for the clinic, hoping to catch Charlie before the end of the day.

"Willow Park Mobile Vet. How may I help you?" a young voice answered.

"Hello. This is Dr. Harjo from the diagnostic lab. Is Dr. Anderson there? It's about Shadowhawk Williams."

"Yes, ma'am. Hold, please. Let me see if I can grab him."

A minute passed before Charlie picked up the line.

"Josie! Good to hear from you. Mr. Williams called me this morning, saying they lost another horse. What do you have for me?"

"Howdy, Charlie. Not a lot, sorry. Rabies testing was negative. The sulfur concentration in the feed was normal. I forwarded the sample to the virology lab for EHV and West Nile testing. I also sent the feed off for fumonisin testing. Histo is pending."

"Thanks, Josie. This is a weird one. Mr. Williams is frantic."

"I imagine so. Quick question: Did you figure out if a necropsy report is required for insurance?"

"Let me check."

I heard Mr. Anderson typing as he pulled up the JW Ranch records.

"They're insured with Green Saddle. Don't know how much for." Charlie paused. "Looks like they only require a vet note and pics. Hope Mr. Williams grabbed those before he buried them." A hint of frustration seeped through his voice.

"I have some pics of Shadowhawk. Let me know if you need them."

"Thanks. Not sure I want to fill out the vet form until I get your report back. This is a weird one. Mr. Williams hasn't been pressing me for it yet. I'll just sit tight. When do you think you'll get a cause of death?"

"Not sure," I said, slightly disappointed in myself. "This is an unusual case. Even Sandy is scratching her head."

Charlie grunted, perplexed himself.

Sandy was a staple in Oklahoma, and all the vets knew her, either having been taught by her in veterinary school or having worked with her during her long tenure. She was a well-respected member of the veterinary community. In a twisted way, I felt better knowing she didn't have an answer either.

"You've been out on the ranch. Any reason anyone would want to kill the horses? Whether out of spite or for the insurance money?" I asked.

Charlie paused before answering. It was a very direct and atypical question. It wasn't often that people maliciously killed the animals they worked with or owned.

"I don't know," he said slowly. "They're an odd bunch out there. And Mr. Williams keeps going on and on about that ranch hand."

"I could order a gagillion tests. But I'm thinking we wait until the onsite visit on Wednesday. Get our eyes on what's going on out there. Will you be joining us?"

"If I can, I will. Depends on if I get any emergencies."

"Great. Looking forward to seeing you, Charlie. It's been a while."

"Same here. Y'all have a good day and keep me posted."

"Yes, sir."

We said our goodbyes, and I hung up the phone.

I leaned back in my chair, tapping my pen on the desk. This case was a bugger. The fact that Adam had buried the other horses without even Charlie getting eyes on them kept nagging at me, especially with some hefty insurance payouts on the line.

After taking a moment to collect my thoughts, I gave Adam a call. It went straight to voicemail. I felt relief followed by guilt for feeling grateful that I wouldn't have to talk to him live. In the message, I informed him of the results to date and reminded him about the ranch visit on Wednesday.

I hung up, feeling sick to my stomach.

* * *

It had been a bumpy day, and coming back home felt like a big hug. After feeding Yersi, I showered, plopped on my couch, and debated eating a real meal. But my depression got the better of me, and I sat with a pint of mocha ice cream, fully intending to polish the entire thing off for dinner. Yersi sat on my lap, purring as if he knew I needed extra TLC today.

About halfway through the pint, my phone binged with a text from Laila.

> Thinking of you. How was the rest of your day

> Lame

> Oh no! What happened?!

> That stupid case. Stress eating ice cream now

> Want to call?

> No

> Thanks though

> Want to crawl into my closet in a fetal position

I inserted a gif of a woman sobbing and stuffing her face with cookies. Laila added a laughing tag.

> Im here if you need me

> TY

> U rock

> Want to do lunch sometime this week?

> Yessssss

> What day?

> Wednesday?

> I have a farm tour that day :(

Another day?

Friday?

That works

McAlisters at noon?

Sounds good

Though I still wasn't a hundred percent, having Laila check on me helped. I'd finish up this pint of ice cream, go water the garden, and hit the hay. The Shadowhawk case might not be solved tomorrow, but an answer should come eventually. I'd just have to keep at it.

CHAPTER
TWELVE

When I came into work on Tuesday, a dead horse was waiting for me.

Dustin was already out on the necropsy floor, and the horse was laid out on the hydraulic table. When I opened the door, a wall of Hank Williams and the sound of Dustin straightening his knife's edge washed over me. Seeing me in my civvies at the door, he gave me a nod in greeting and walked over.

"Mornin', Doc," he said in greeting but didn't smile. My stomach clenched.

"Hey, Dustin." I tilted my chin towards the horse. "What's the deal with that one?"

"Racehorse." He pulled the paperwork from the hanging file organizer bolted into the wall next to the door and handed it to me.

I let out an audible sigh of relief.

"At least it's not another neuro horse from that same place as last week," Dustin said.

"Well, that's assuming he'd even bring the body in if another one died," I snarked, surprising myself with the bitterness in my voice.

Dustin snorted in reply and shook his head. He'd seen it all.

I felt myself starting to blame the rancher even though I didn't have anything to suggest he was involved. Somehow, a seed of distrust in

Adam had been sown, and I felt it growing. Dustin seemed to be leaning in that direction, too. Deep down, I hoped the guy hadn't killed his horses to collect the insurance money.

"Welp, let's knock this puppy out. Let me get changed, and I'll be right back." Despite the black cloud of the Shadowhawk case, I was eager to get 'er done.

"Roger that," Dustin said, dipping his head again before going back to straightening the edge of his blade.

Back out on the floor, I dove right in. The patient was a three-year-old thoroughbred from the racetrack. It'd broken its front leg during practice and had been euthanized. My job was to document the injuries. A researcher on campus was looking into the different types of fractures the horses received while racing, hoping to prevent injuries in the future. I'd also need to collect joint fluid for drug testing, which was required by the Thoroughbred Racing Association of Oklahoma; they had a zero-tolerance doping policy.

"Can you grab pics while I collect the joint samples?" I asked.

"Yes, ma'am. I have the tubes labeled for you already." He handed me several redtop tubes labeled with the accession number and joints from which the fluid would be collected.

I tossed him a smile. "Thanks, dude."

He nodded and grabbed the camera. He quickly took pictures of the horse's identifying marks for the insurance company. He also took pictures of the right front leg. There was a complete fracture of the lower cannon bone that had broken through the skin. That was the money-maker right there and would take most of my time.

With the external examination and initial sample collection complete, we settled into the routine of opening the carcass. Moving in tandem, we made quick work of the internal organs, which were squeaky clean, as expected.

Dustin sawed off the right front leg and stripped the skin. I captured additional pictures of the exposed fracture, took measurements, and jotted down notes. It felt good to be buried in the routine of working on a case with a clear-cut answer, even if the case itself was sad.

As if reading my thoughts, Dustin said, "Racehorse injuries are depressing."

I nodded slowly, feeling my lips tighten.

"Doesn't seem fair that injured football players get to retire and horses with the same thing get sent to the pearly gates." He shook his head.

"Yeah," I sighed. "But how would you even treat something like that?" I gestured to the fracture; the two pieces of shattered bone were held together by shredded muscle and a strip of skin. "Sure, an injury like that in a person, they'd have to amputate it. But you can't amputate a horse's leg like you can in dogs and cats. Plus, it's not like they have prosthetics or wheelchairs for horses."

"I guess," Dustin said, doubtful. "I don't mind killing animals to eat. But seeing them die for entertainment...." He shrugged again.

I gave him a side nudge of support. I agreed, but all the two of us could do at this moment in time was support the research that was leading to advancements in horseshoe structure and tract substrates that reduced injuries in equine athletes.

* * *

With the racehorse case quickly buttoned up, I was out of my coveralls and back at my desk before 10 A.M. I was pecking away at my computer, writing the report when my phone rang.

"Dr. Harjo. How can I help you?" I answered.

"Dr. Harjo. This is James. I have an officer on the line for you."

"Huh?" I blurted, surprised. I seldom got calls from the police. When I did, it was because I was working on a pretty serious legal case they had submitted directly. I hadn't had a case like that in ages.

"Office Watts is on the line for you, ma'am," James said. "Want me to transfer him through or send him to voicemail?"

"Go ahead and transfer him," I answered, heart thudding.

I heard two clicks before James came back on. "Officer Watts?"

"Yes," a deep, masculine voice replied.

"I have Dr. Harjo on the line for you."

"Thank you," the officer replied as James clicked off.

"Hello, Officer Watts. This is Dr. Josie Harjo. How can I help you?" I asked, feeling nervous and not understanding why.

"Hello, Dr. Harjo. I'm the officer working an assault case and would like to ask you some questions."

Assault? What the fuck?

"Sure, I'll answer as best as I can. Is this related to one of my cases?" I probed, grasping at straws; assault wasn't a word used in non-human species, and I was at a loss as to why he was calling *me*.

"Yes, ma'am. I have information that you may be handling a case related to a dead horse from JW Ranch."

Oh fuck, oh fuck, oh fuck.

"Yes, sir," was all I could get out as my voice caught in my throat.

Residency programs taught you how to do a necropsy, write a report, and pass the board exam. We didn't learn squat about how to testify in court or talk to the police, probably because it rarely happened. I was completely out of my element.

"Do you have any information that you can share with me about that case?" he asked.

I cleared my throat to buy myself a moment to think. We normally weren't allowed to share information about a case with anyone but the person who submitted it unless granted permission from that same person. The cops were different.

"We don't know much at this point," I answered carefully. "I've ruled out rabies, but that testing set us back a few days. There are a lot of other potential viral and toxicological causes. We're working our way down the list."

"Any chance the horse was murdered?"

My stomach clenched, and my brows furrowed. "That's…that's an odd question." I grabbed my pen and started fidgeting with it. "We usually don't talk about animals being murdered." I stopped there, hoping he'd fill the space with more background.

"I'm just curious if you found anything to suggest malicious behavior," he pressed. "Any external wounds or evidence of bruising?"

"I haven't found anything to suggest that someone purposefully abused or killed the horse if that's what you're asking. Is there something I should be looking for?" I pushed back.

"Mrs. Williams has filed assault charges against a former employee. When we were out there, she insisted that he killed several of their horses. Mr. Williams gave us your name. I'm following up to see if there is any connection."

Holy shit.

"What happened at the ranch?" I asked.

"I'm not at liberty to share that information," he said gruffly.

"Can you tell me if this happened recently? I'm trying to build a timeline myself." I knew I was toeing the line, but I couldn't help it.

Giving in a tad, he said, "The alleged altercation occurred on Sunday."

"Right before the fourth horse died?" I blurted.

"What?" he said with surprise.

"Mr. Williams left a message on my voicemail on Monday morning saying they'd found another horse dead."

The silence stretched between us.

"Officer Watts?" I asked, unsure if the call had dropped.

"Yes, ma'am. Just taking notes," he said.

My eyebrows shot up in surprise. I realized that the death of the fourth horse was news to him. If I'd been Adam, I would've called the police as soon as I found another dead animal, and I'd bet just about any other rancher would have, too. I couldn't help but think he was trying to hide something.

Wanting to make sure Office Watts had the full picture, I added, "They had two deaths prior to Friday last week. I'm not sure when, and they buried those horses. The vet, Dr. Charlie Anderson from Willow Park, came out Friday when the third one died. That's the horse we received. The fourth was also buried."

I could practically hear the wheels turning in his head as he took it all in.

"Do you know why they didn't bring the other horses in?"

"No, sir."

"How often do people bring in multiple dead animals?" he asked.

"It depends. If animals are insured, they usually bring them in for necropsy." I felt myself relaxing; I could talk about veterinary medicine until the cows came home.

"The horses are insured?" he interrupted, surprise lacing his voice.

"Yes, sir. And it's my understanding that the horses at JW Ranch are highly valuable." I paused. "And that's the other thing that's kinda odd. Usually, in outbreak situations with highly valuable animals, the owners are desperate to figure out what's going on and will bring in each one that dies, especially when we don't get a clear answer on the first animal they bring in. More bodies mean a better chance of solving the case."

"Do you know when you'll have the cause of death?" he asked.

"No, sir. I suspect it will take a week or more." I started anxiously tapping my pen on my desk and chewed my cheek. I couldn't escape the feeling of ineptitude, no matter how invalid it might be.

"Can you please keep me posted?" It felt like a demand rather than a polite question.

"Yes, sir. Is there something in particular I should be looking for?" I asked again.

"Not that I'm aware of. But I'll give you a jingle if I get any more information," he said, a little less cagey.

"Thank you," I answered. "Every little bit helps."

He left his number with me before we said polite goodbyes.

After hanging up, I leaned back in my chair, my pen still tapping on the desk as I mulled the case over. People frequently thought someone killed their pet, but nine times out of ten, it was a natural cause of death. Sandy's voice echoed in my head: *If you hear hoofbeats, think horses, not zebra*s. After the call with the officer, I was thinking this might just be a zebra.

* * *

Trying to shake off the foreboding feeling from my call with Officer Watts, I grabbed my lunch and headed to the breakroom. I needed to step away from the Shadowhawk case for a bit and recenter.

Anna and Dustin were seated at a table with Carol from the front office. Happy to see some of my favorite people sitting together, I grabbed the fourth seat.

"Howdy, Dr. Harjo," Dustin said, scooching his meal over so I had room to unpack my lunch next to him.

"Hey, y'all." I unpacked my homemade salad and container of almonds.

"Oh, dear. How do you not just die of starvation?" Carol asked.

Carol had been at the lab for over forty years. Past retirement age, she was the most seasoned veteran on staff. She also had the biggest heart and looked after everyone.

I laughed. "I'll be fine. There's lots of good stuff in here." I held the salad out to Carol, showing her all of the fruit and veggies from my garden that topped the lettuce.

"You eat like a rabbit, sweety. You gotta take care of yourself." She reached across the table and patted my hand.

"Yes, ma'am," I said politely with a smile.

Carol's heart was in the right place. She thought that fried chicken, biscuits and gravy, and bacon were the three major food groups, with ice cream being next in line. She always brought amazing chilis, stews, and various baked goods to share. Though I could eat the occasional bowl of deer chili, especially when Dustin made it, all of that greasy food never sat right with me. I felt better if I ate fresh food straight from the garden.

Carol held out a container of cookies. "Want one?"

The smell of chocolate chip bar cookies wafted across the table, and my mouth watered. Even though it was the simplest of cookies, Carol's chocolate chip bar cookies were unbeatable.

Unable to resist, I answered, "Sure, thanks."

I took one cookie and laid it on the top of my napkin for dessert, secretly congratulating myself on my restraint. In reality, I wanted fifteen of them.

Digging into my salad, I asked Anna and Dustin, "Anything else come in?"

Anna shook her head as Dustin said, "No, ma'am."

My shoulders sagged with relief. Dustin noticed and smiled knowingly.

Carol and Anna picked up their conversation on barrel racing as I dug into my salad. It was nice to let my mind relax with casual chatter.

As the conversation shifted to the upcoming football season, James walked in. He dragged a fifth chair to join us at the table and set his lunchbox down. James was about a year out of high school, but he did an amazing job handling the calls coming into the lab. Carol had taken him under her wing, imparting her immense knowledge to her eager pupil.

"Oh, my gosh, Dr. Harjo. What did the police officer want?" James drawled, eager for the gossip.

Anna and Dustin's eyebrows went up. Carol was unfazed, probably because she'd already heard the news. That, and she'd seen just about everything in her forty-plus-year tenure at the lab.

"Police?" Dustin asked, unable to hide his surprise.

"Yeah, a cop called me earlier about the Shadowhawk case," I answered, suddenly not feeling hungry anymore.

"Is that the horse from last Friday?" Anna asked.

"Yep," I sighed.

"Why is a police officer calling you about a dead horse?" Dustin asked, just as confused as I was when I got the call.

I shrugged. "I guess the ranch hand—the one they were complaining about—he assaulted one of the owners this weekend... allegedly."

Everyone around the table stared at me, waiting for me to continue.

"Anyway, the cop just wanted to know if the death of the horse was suspicious," I added.

"Pshh." Dustin waved his hand. "Owners always say that."

"Yeah." I shook my head slowly. "But something is off about this case...I don't know."

"Ohhhh," Carol said with a mix of eagerness and shock. "You think the horse was killed?"

She loved a good mystery. But she was also so kind-hearted that it was difficult for her to believe that someone would be cruel enough to kill a horse.

I shrugged in reply. If I'd been asked before that phone call, I probably would've laughed at the question. Now, a seed of doubt had been sown, and I couldn't entirely rule out the possibility that something more nefarious had happened.

"Do you know why the horse died?" Anna asked.

"Not yet, sadly," I answered. I took a bite of my salad, uncomfortable with the direction the conversation was drifting.

Dustin frowned. "The weird thing is they've had four horses die, but they only brought in the one."

"Huh," Anna mused. "That *is* weird. He brought in the feed and water right away. Why didn't he bring in the other horses?"

"No clue," I answered, frustrated. "We may never know. All we can do is try to solve the case that he did bring in."

"We should get the herpes and West Nile results back today," Dustin offered.

"Yeah. I'll check on that after lunch. I'll also get the histo back in a day or two, and we're going to the ranch tomorrow. I'm starting to think it's a toxin or a poisoning, but those cases can take a while to figure out. Hopefully, we can button this up quickly."

Dustin grunted in sympathy.

The conversation shifted to lighter things, and I started to shake off the unease from the phone call.

As we were packing up to go, Dustin leaned over and said low enough that only I could hear, "Don't worry too much. It'll all get sorted."

I flashed him a smile as we shared a knuckle bump.

* * *

I was starting to feel better until Gerald decided to shit on the whole thing.

As I was walking back to my office, he called from behind me. I briefly toyed with the idea of ignoring him, dashing to my office, and slamming the door in his face. Unable to be that rude, I turned to face him and forced a smile.

"Hello, Gerald," I said with a stiff voice.

"I heard that you got a call from the police," he said in a self-satisfied tone. He crossed his arms and, no joke, puffed up his chest.

Good Lord, news travels fast.

I tried not to roll my eyes.

"Yes," I said, not offering any more information. He'd have to pry the facts from my cold dead hands.

"Why are the police calling you?" His eyes flashed eagerly. He was practically rubbing his hands together like Mr. Burns.

I could feel the irritation building; I was pretty sure he wanted to see me go down in burning flames.

"It's about a case," I answered curtly.

His posture instantly changed. Despite my slightly rude tone, his shoulders relaxed, and his eyes lit up with genuine interest.

"Oh," was all he said. After a beat, he added, "Anything I can help with?"

He was so oblivious to social cues that I couldn't help but shake my head.

"No thanks. I have it under control," I lied.

His shoulders sank further, and now, he almost looked like a sad puppy.

"Which case is it?" he needled.

"Four horses have died out at JW Ranch," I shared, knowing he'd go back to his office and dig up the information anyway.

"What did you find on necropsy?"

I tried not to groan. The last thing I wanted to be doing was talking to Gerald Richter in the fucking hallway about an unsolved case that was keeping me up at night.

"There were no gross lesions." Anticipating the questions that would follow, I added, "Rabies was negative. Virology, toxicology, and histology are pending."

I could practically see his mind whirling, trying to solve the case. "I'm certain it's herpes."

Biting back a snort at his fervent conviction, I said, "Well, that's one of several differentials. I'm going to check now to see if the virology results are back."

His eyes lit up again, and I knew he'd be racing me back to see who could pull the results up first.

"Anything else?" I asked, irritated.

He shook his head and moved briskly past me to his office without another word.

What the fuck?

Resisting the competitive urge, I tried to shrug off the encounter and headed to my office at a normal pace. I slid into my chair, woke my computer, and logged in to check the virology results.

Staring at my screen in disappointment, I rested back in my chair. The brain sample was negative for both herpesvirus and West Nile virus.

Damn.

Since the horses were vaccinated, I'd expected these results deep down. But I couldn't help feeling an ounce of hope that I might make this case go away without any more calls from the cops. Now, those hopes were dashed, and I'd been pushed into the vast world of toxicology. Whether accidental or intentional, I'd need to start working my way through the myriad toxins that could take out a quarter of a herd on a ranch.

To make matters worse, I'd have to look the owners in the eye tomorrow and tell them I had no clue what the hell was going on at JW Ranch.

CHAPTER
THIRTEEN

It was field trip day, and I couldn't help but feel like it was a do-or-die moment.

I hadn't realized how nervous I was until I woke up ahead of the alarm, my stomach in knots. I'd done several site visits in my tenure as a pathologist, but I'd never felt this confusing mixture of curiosity and dread.

I pulled myself out of bed to an annoyed *merf* from Yersi and went through the motions of getting ready, head still foggy. Knowing we'd be walking around a ranch, I dressed in a casual blouse, fitted jeans, and hand-made cowboy boots. My hair was pulled back in a ponytail and tucked beneath a baseball cap. For good luck, I wore matching beaded earrings and a thick bracelet Aunty had given me, not the pair from last weekend, but an older set with bright red and yellow patterns.

After making sure Yersi and the chickens were settled, I filled my thermos with extra black tea. It was time to toughen up and face Mr. Williams.

* * *

I arrived at the lab early and made it to my office without any run-ins with Gerald. I was already feeling a dose of anxiety with a dash of self-doubt; seeing that jerk was the last thing I needed today.

When the clock hit 8 A.M., I went hunting for Dustin before I headed out. The necropsy floor was empty, the starched smell of cleaning chemicals hitting me when I leaned through the door. Instead, I found him perched at his desk, scrolling on his phone, coffee cup steaming by his computer.

"Mornin'," I said.

"Hey, Doc," Dustin answered.

"No cases, I assume?"

"No, ma'am."

"Cool. I'm going out to the ranch—where the neuro horse was from—with Sandy today. Text me if something urgent comes in. Otherwise, I'll check back in the afternoon."

He brought his hand to his brow, acknowledging the request with a friendly salute. "I'll be here."

I headed to the receiving department, grabbed the keys for the lab truck, and signed them out. I ducked past Gerald's office to find Sandy. She was all ready to go, wearing her own set of jeans and boots, cowboy hat in hand. Greeting me with a smile, she grabbed her pack, gave a heads-up to the toxicology techs, and followed me out to the truck.

"Let's do this," she said.

Her confidence was infectious, and I loved her for it.

I grabbed the driver's seat, and she took shotgun. The lab truck was a white, two-cylinder pick-up. It ran low to the ground, and the gas mileage was crap. But it worked well enough for most errands and site visits. I hoped JW Ranch had a well-maintained driveway. Otherwise, we'd be hoofing it from the main road.

Deciding to throw caution to the wind, we rolled down the windows and let the cool morning air flow through the cabin. It was a pleasant thirty-minute drive to the ranch. The roads were virtually empty, and the sky was clear and bright. Prairie stretched off in either direction with speckles of cattle breaking the endless waves of native grass pastures.

JW Ranch was along an isolated stretch of a two-lane asphalt road. Large pastures stretched to either side. The buildings were tucked far back from the main road behind a looming metal gate with the ranch name and logo.

I pulled through the open gate and onto the bumpy gravel driveway. Blood-red clumps of dried mud formed thick borders between the gravel and the adjacent pasture. Thankfully, the gravel portion of the driveway was well-maintained, and I was feeling pretty good that the little truck would make it okay.

To the left of the driveway, cattle grazed in the tall grass of the far pasture that was bordered by barbed wire. To the right, there was a large, fenced sand arena with an adjacent, smaller lunge arena. A huge, enclosed barn sat beyond that, which was likely where the horses were stalled. Further down the road was a pole barn stuffed with towering bales. At the end of the road, a gloomy, two-story house hunkered, standing watch. Looking at it, I felt the hair on the back of my neck prickle.

Charlie's large work truck was already parked in front of the horse barn, marked by a large veterinary caduceus and his clinic name. He was sitting behind the wheel, poking at his phone, as I pulled in next to him. Seeing the movement, he looked up and waved. The three of us climbed out of our trucks and gathered in front of the barn.

The sun was fully up, and the humid heat pressed in. The incessant buzzing of cicadas clogged the air. Sandy put her hat on, and I pulled my cap down to shade my eyes better.

Seeing Charlie, I couldn't help but smile. "Nice seeing you again, Charlie." I reached out to shake his hand.

"Likewise," he answered before turning to Sandy. "Sandy," he said with a nod as he took her hand next.

"Appreciate you takin' the time. How's business?" Sandy asked.

"It's been pretty darn busy. I've been bustin' my tail. After the calving season, things usually slow down a bit. Not so much this year. I lucked out and had an opening this morning. This case has been a head-scratcher for me. Figured this would be an opportunity to see you work your magic and also give me a chance to get an eye on the other horses."

"Yeah, I've been gnawing my fingernails over the rest of the horses," I agreed.

He leaned in and lowered his voice. "Real quick—Mr. and Mrs. Williams are a little unusual, especially Sue. Y'all just gotta roll with it." He drew his lips in a line and nodded slightly to himself, feeling better at having imparted the warning.

Sandy nodded back, apparently unphased. Anxiety crept back into my stomach. I didn't want anyone all up in my face today.

Returning to his normal volume, Charlie said in a cheery voice, "Shall we, then? Mr. Williams is in the barn."

Sandy and I followed Charlie into the enclosed barn, gravel crunching under our feet until we stepped onto the poured cement floors.

The barn was pretty snazzy. Everything was freshly painted and well-maintained. The tack was neatly organized in a niche off to the right. Next to the tack was a small alcove for feed storage. There was a seating area with a small fridge and a counter with snacks. The pleasant scent of horses and alfalfa filled the barn. I inhaled, loving the smell.

Adam had one of the horses out, lead rope tied to the stall door, and was brushing it down. He looked up as we walked in, and I couldn't help but notice his back stiffening. He put the brush down and came over, hands on his hips. He met us near the entrance and tipped his hat.

"Mornin', Mr. Williams," Charlie said with a friendly smile and shook Adam's hand. Charlie had a way about him, and I admired his ability to be friendly to the oddest of folks.

"Hello again, Mr. Williams." I shook his hand before turning to Sandy. "This is Dr. Sandy Bishop, the toxicologist."

Adam shook her hand with a polite nod before stepping back and looping his thumbs in his belt. "I assume since y'all are here that you don't have an answer for me."

His tone and body language were hard to read, and I wasn't sure how to take that comment. It felt accusatory, but there was a bit of smugness about him that just didn't fit.

Sandy jumped in and said, "Sometimes, our job is more about ruling things out."

I sent a silent *thank you* to Sandy.

I jumped in: "I'm not sure if you've had a chance to read through the recent results, but the viral testing has come back negative. So, in addition to blister beetle and rabies, we've also ruled out herpesvirus and West Nile virus."

"That still doesn't tell me what's killing my horses," he said, crossing his arms.

"After ruling out some of the more common infectious cases, I'm leaning toward a toxicity," I said, starting to feel backed into a corner.

"When are you gonna know what poison was used?" Adam pressed.

Sandy and I couldn't help trading a glance.

"We can blow a ton of money fumbling in the dark trying to figure out which toxin or poison it is," I continued. "I'm hoping our visit today will help narrow it down. If not, looking at the samples under the microscope will help. We won't get the slides back for a while, though."

Adam's face started to flush, and his lips pressed in a tight line. Out of the corner of my eye, I saw Charlie start to fidget.

"It's Ben. I'm sure of it. He killed my horses." Adam let out an angry huff.

"We aren't sure what caused the deaths yet," I said, trying to keep my voice calm, though I felt myself start to sweat. "And, even if we determine the cause, it'll be up to the police to figure out who did it if it looks like the poisoning was intentional."

Adam scowled at me, and I had to force myself not to take a small step back. I could tell this was going sideways fast. Owners who've lost a treasured or valuable animal could get angry, but there was a whole other level of aggression wafting off of him.

Sensing the building tension, Charlie came in to save the day.

"Most of the time, deaths like these are accidental, Mr. Williams. How 'bout you show us around?"

Adam shifted a bit and then nodded slightly. He uncrossed his arms, but his shoulders stayed tense.

"Which stall was Shadowhawk in again?" Charlie asked. I was sure Charlie knew exactly where the horse had been kept, and I appreciated his efforts to help redirect Adam.

Adam led us over to an empty stall near the back of the barn. Charlie chatted him up as Sandy and I nosed around. The bedding in the stall had been thoroughly removed, and the stall appeared to have been extensively scrubbed.

That was quick.

I couldn't tell if the action of washing everything away helped dampen the despair or if they were trying to hide something.

I walked the stall perimeter and squatted down, running my fingers over some deep gouges in the wood panels. I looked up at Sandy with my eyebrows raised. Sandy subtly nodded back. I was certain these were hoof marks from the horse thrashing, further evidence of a struggle before death.

Sandy walked over to investigate the automatic waterer. The waterer was full of what appeared to be clean water. She pressed the paddle, and it filled as expected. Given that the water came from the city line, it was unlikely to be a natural contamination, and a steady flow made dehydration unlikely. The water would be easy to poison, though. With no other water source, the horse would be forced to drink it even if it smelled or tasted funny.

With minimal information collected from the turn about the inside of the stall, Sandy and I rejoined Charlie and Adam.

"Can you show us the stalls from the other horses who passed?" I asked.

"Sure," Adam replied, starting to fidget.

The stalls from the other dead horses were randomly scattered around the barn. I peeked into the other occupied stalls along the way. The remaining horses looked relaxed, often snoozing with a back leg cocked. The stalls were filled with a generous layer of well-maintained wood shavings. All of the waterers looked to be functioning. The barn was almost peaceful. It was hard to imagine that four dramatic deaths had happened in this building in the last week.

The stalls that had housed the other dead horses were similar to Shadowhawk's. All of the bedding had been removed, and they were scrubbed clean, almost as if to erase what had happened. This little detail nagged at me.

Charlie had done a great job keeping Adam occupied with idle chatter, moving him to the front of the barn as Sandy and I nosed around. Little tells, like anxious glances and picking at his fingers, told me that Adam was uncomfortable with the whole situation.

What's got you so worried, Mr. Williams?

Sandy and I circled back to the front of the barn to join them.

"Ready to see the pole barn?" Charlie asked.

"Mind if I take a look at where the bagged feed is stored first?" Sandy asked.

Adam's eyes shifted nervously. "Sure. We store it all here." He gestured to the stacks inside the small alcove.

The storage area for the bagged feed was clean and dry. The bags were stored above floor level on a layer of pallets. Amazingly, there was no evidence of rodent feces or holes in any of the bags. They didn't look like they had been wet or tampered with, either.

"May I open one?" Sandy asked.

Adam popped open his knife with a click, startling me. He passed by me, selected a bag, and sliced it open. He returned his knife to his pocket.

Sandy dipped her hands in the feed, running it through her fingers. Her lips pursed, but she stayed silent.

"Thank you," Sandy said. "You may want to stop feeding the pelleted feed until we can make sure it's safe."

"That's what Doc Harjo said. We've only been feeding the baled alfalfa since Monday." Adam grabbed some duct tape, sealed the bag, and leaned it against the stack.

"Do you keep any chemicals in here?" Sandy asked.

"Like rat bait?" Adam replied.

"Yeah, like rat bait, wood stain, pesticides, anything like that." She kept her body posture relaxed, but her eyes were intent on Adam.

Adam started to pick at his fingers again.

"I think you store some things over there. Right, Mr. Williams?" Charlie nudged, pointing to the cabinets under the sink in the seating area.

"Yes, sir," Adam said, sounding cagey.

Sandy took the initiative and explored the cabinet under the sink. I followed her, peering over her shoulder. Charlie was a gem and once again kept Adam occupied. I couldn't help but notice the continued side-eye. The dude was jumpy.

Sandy pulled out a couple of bottles. "This is like a poison control center poster." She stood and pointed to a bottle of slug bait. "That right there has metaldehyde in it." Her finger moved to point to a bottle of gopher bait. "And that has zinc phosphide in it. Both of them can cause neurologic disease in horses."

"Holy shit, Sandy," I said under my breath. She nodded.

Slug and gopher bait poisoning were both rare in horses. I racked my brain, trying to remember the lesions associated with these toxicities. I had a niggly thought that had something to do with pale livers in horses who had eaten gopher bait. But I couldn't recall if slug bait had any gross lesions.

"The rest of the stuff is toxic, but I'm less worried about those." She waved her hand at the other bottles and metal cans under the sink.

I whipped my phone out and took a quick picture, hoping Adam hadn't noticed.

Sandy turned to Charlie and Adam. "Would y'all mind coming over here for a sec?"

Once they were standing next to us, Sandy continued, "Both of these baits can be toxic to horses. I'd recommend tossing them. But, if you are going to use them on your property, I recommend storing them in your garage and not applying them anywhere near the horses or the cattle."

"Is that what killed them?" Adam asked, his face a mask.

Sandy shrugged. "Have you used either of these chemicals recently?"

"No, ma'am. But Ben sure could have," Adam answered angrily.

The tension was building again, and I felt uncomfortable being this close to Adam. The memory of the click of the knife made me jittery.

"We can test for both of these compounds in the samples that Dr. Harjo collected," Sandy said. "It's a send-out test, so it will take a bit. But we'll get that ordered as soon as we get back to the lab. Until then, I'd just toss them out to be safe."

"That's what killed them, then?" Adam pressed.

Charlie stepped in and said, "We won't know until we get the test results back, Mr. Williams. Dr. Bishop and Dr. Harjo are doing their best to get this figured out for you."

Adam pursed his lips.

"Let's go have a look at the alfalfa now," Sandy said.

As they were leaving the barn, an older woman approached from the house. She was lean with leathered skin and permanent frown lines. She looked like she'd been through some tough times but had survived through sheer force of will.

"You the lab people?" she asked with a bitter, gravelly voice.

"Yes, ma'am. I'm Dr. Josie Harjo, and this is Dr. Sandy Bishop." I stuck my hand out to shake, and the woman ignored me.

"You're not like real doctors, though." The woman tutted. "Have you got an answer yet? We got insurance paperwork to fill out."

Sandy and I exchanged another glance. The woman was so curt that it was borderline aggressive. There was also a hint of nastiness that rubbed me the wrong way.

"It's probably the slug bait or the gopher bait," Adam said in a neutral tone. He flashed the woman a look that sure felt a heck of a lot like a warning.

"We're not sure yet, Mrs. Williams," Charlie chimed in.

Feeling emboldened, I jumped in, "We ruled out common viral infections and blister beetles."

"I could have told you it wasn't those things," Sue interrupted, crossing her arms. "We only buy the best alfalfa, and all our animals are vaccinated."

What the hell? Why is she so defensive?

Trying to wade through the wave of hostility, I added, "I'm leaning toward a toxicity. Slug and gopher bait are possibilities since they're onsite, but it could be something like a toxic plant or mold."

"Did the police call you?" Mrs. Williams barked, ignoring what I said.

Scrambling to shift gears, I replied, "Uh…yes, ma'am."

Charlie was unable to cover the flash of surprise that crossed his face.

"Did they tell you that Ben was here on Sunday?" Sue growled.

"Officer Watts didn't provide any details," I said, secretly hoping she would fill in the blanks.

She obliged. "I fired him and said we'd mail his last paycheck. He showed up Sunday, drunk, demanding to be paid in cash. I told him to leave, but he started throwing things around the barn, scaring the horses. When he pushed me to the ground, I wasn't gonna take none of that no more. I had to pull my gun to get 'em to leave."

Adam flashed her another warning glance. I tucked that little detail away with the others. Did Officer Watts know about that nugget? There was some bad blood between these folks.

"We found Twilight Messenger dead the next morning," she continued. "He's just killing the horses to get back at us." Her face filled with rage.

"We'll figure this out, Mrs. Williams. And, if it looks malicious, we'll make sure those who are responsible pay," Charlie chimed in, trying to dampen the climbing tension.

Slightly mollified, she gave a tense nod.

"We were about to head over to the haybarn," Charlie continued. "Would you like to join us?"

Not much fazed good 'ole Charlie. I sent him an appreciative glance.

Mrs. Williams grunted, released her crossed arms, and stomped over to the haybarn, the rest of us following behind. At the front of the barn, she waved her arms in a "there you go" way, almost dismissively, and crossed them again. Charlie kept the Williamses occupied at the front of the barn while Sandy and I navigated through the stacked bales.

"What the hell was that?" I whispered to Sandy. "I've never seen an owner flip out like that before."

Sandy sucked her teeth. "No clue. But I suggest we get a look-see and get the heck out of dodge."

Trying to shake the spooked feeling, I focused on investigating the bales. The barn was fairly large with a cement floor and, like everything else on the property, was well-maintained. Enough bales of alfalfa to last through the winter were neatly stacked on top of wood pallets. The nearest section had bales arranged in steps and was the stack they'd been feeding from. A scruffy, tabby barn cat lounged on one of the intact bales, letting out a raspy *meow* as we approached. I reached down and scratched its chin.

I asked, "Anything?"

"No," Sandy said. "I didn't see any toxic plants poking out, and the alfalfa doesn't look moldy. But that's not saying much. Let's open some up."

She grabbed a pair of cutters lying next to the bales and snipped the wires on two bales. They fluffed open like an accordion, and she picked through the flakes.

"Looks clean," Sandy said, shaking her head. "I don't think it's the alfalfa."

Noticing Sandy scanning the floor, I asked, "What are you looking for?"

She shrugged one shoulder. "You never know what you'll find if you look. I'm also checking if they use the baits around the barn. But I don't see anything worrisome."

We wove back through the barn to the front.

"What'd you find?" Charlie asked, thumbs hooked casually in his belt loops.

"I don't think it's the alfalfa," Sandy answered. "It's pretty good quality."

"Of course, it is," Sue snarked.

"I didn't see any mold, blister beetles, or toxic plants," Sandy continued, ignoring the interruption. "I think you're okay to keep feeding the alfalfa for now."

"Do the horses ever go out on pasture?" I asked. I'd thrown the question to Adam before, but it never hurt to confirm, especially with Sue there.

"No, ma'am," Adam answered.

"I don't think we need to walk the pastures then," I said, catching Sandy's eye to confirm. "Do the horses get any treats? Ever feed them any clippings from the yard?"

"The ranch hands will feed them carrots sometimes. But nothin' else," Adam replied.

"Thanks, Mr. Williams," I said, trying to be polite, even though he gave me the creeps. "Anything else, Sandy?"

Sandy pursed her lips and shook her head.

"We'll get outta your hair, then," Charlie chimed in, nodding to the parked trucks down the drive.

"That ain't gonna do." Sue's voice was low and angry. "Adam was telling me we've already racked up a bill of a thousand dollars. Now, you're telling me you come out here sniffing around and ain't got no answers? This ranch is about ready to fold. We need the insurance money to pay *your* bill!" She pointed her finger at me, accusatory.

What the hell? I turned to Sandy, surprised by the outburst.

"Ben did this to us," she continued, voice rising. "It's probably that bait. Just fill out the damn forms for us so we can put this behind us. You tell the police what's what."

Sandy's eyebrows shot up at the display, and I bristled. I was already lashing myself with guilt for not having an answer for them. I didn't need this drama on top of everything else.

"If I see Ben again, I'll kill him," she hissed.

Trying to diffuse the situation, Charlie put his hands up and said, "Now, now. Everyone's doing their best."

Adam put his hand on her shoulder. She tensed, crossed her arms, and fumed.

Charlie coughed uncomfortably and turned to Adam. "Thanks for having us out." He reached out his hand to shake. "We'll leave you to it."

Taking our cue, Sandy and I said curt goodbyes to Adam. Sue glared at us with a deep frown as we walked back to the trucks.

CHAPTER
FOURTEEN

Out from under Sue's furious gaze and within the shelter between our trucks, Sandy, Charlie, and I quickly huddled.

"Sorry 'bout that," Charlie said, slightly embarrassed. "Sue's difficult. Don't take it personally. I saved her dog's leg once after they'd accidentally hit him with the tractor, and she cursed at me. She's just like that."

"It's all good," I said, trying to reassure him but not meaning it. Sue was a live wire, and I'd be thanking my lucky stars if I never crossed paths with her again. Somehow, I felt like she wasn't done with me, though.

"You two thinking it's one of those baits?" Charlie said doubtfully.

"I'm not so sure," Sandy answered. "It doesn't feel right."

"Don't think I've ever seen a horse die from bait before." Charlie mused.

"For what it's worth, I've never heard about either one of them causing outbreaks in horses," I added. "There are rare reports of horses dying from bait, but it'd be awfully hard for the horses here to get access to it unless it was intentional. I'll still order the tests just 'cause it came up. But I don't want to put all our eggs in that basket."

Charlie nodded. "Well, thank you again for coming out here." He reached out his hand to shake.

I clasped it and replied, "Thank you for running interference. Glad you could join us. It would've been pretty darn rough without you. I'll keep you posted."

He shook with Sandy and hopped in his truck.

I knocked the red Oklahoma soil off my boots and climbed into the lab truck. A wall of heat washed out of the cab from being parked in the sun. Sandy blasted the AC as soon as the truck was running.

As we approached the main road, I was forced to pull to the far side of the driveway to let a delivery truck in. As it passed, Sandy and I both caught the logo of the feed supply company on the side.

"That was fast," Sandy mused. "Looks like they ordered new feed already. Glad they were listening."

After letting the truck by, I pulled out onto the main road. "That was the most uncomfortable field trip I've ever been on."

Sandy huffed a laugh. "Yeah, it's up there for me, too."

"Did you notice those scuff marks in the stalls? I'm pretty sure the horses were either in severe pain or having seizures at the end. Given the lack of gross lesions, I'm still leaning toward neurological disease."

"Yep, I agree." Sandy started counting off on her fingers. "There are four horses dead in a week, the deaths happen following little to no clinical signs, and viral disease has been ruled out. It's gotta be a toxicity. I know I always teach if you hear hoofbeats, think of horses, not zebras, but this might actually be a zebra." She patted her hand on her thigh and gazed out the window.

"Being in stalls, the horses can't get into too much, though." I chewed the inside of my cheek.

"Yeah, I don't think it's the water or the alfalfa. Could be the bagged feed."

"Like fumonisin?" I asked. "The bags looked in good shape, and the storage space was neat. It doesn't have the typical look of moldy feed."

"It could have been wet or moldy before processing, though."

Sandy pursed her lips and then waved the thought away. "We'll have to wait on that test."

"I didn't see any toxic plants on the farm, not even out by the house. Did you?"

"Nothing obvious. I had a case once where some people fed oleander trimmings to the ponies next door, thinking they were being nice and not knowing any better. After that humdinger, I always keep an eye out for the ornamentals, like oleander or yew. But I didn't see any."

"Back to the bait. Have you ever seen anyone intentionally poison an animal with that stuff?"

She shook her head. "Other than the guy with the Holsteins, the only case I had of intentional poisoning was someone mixing rat bait in hamburger meat and throwing it over the fence to kill the neighbor's dog. It happened so fast that the rat bait pellets were still obvious in the stomach contents." She patted her hand on her leg again. "Oh. And there was that one case when they fed strychnine to a bunch of birds at an old folks' home. Not sure if that counts." She sighed and started picking at her jeans.

"What about the ranch hand? I know the owners are all wrapped around the axle about him, but...I'm not feeling it." I shrugged one shoulder with my hands still on the wheel.

"It's more likely the owners poisoned the horses for the insurance money," Sandy mused. "The feed prices have been hurting all of the ranchers these days. Mrs. Williams was acting pretty shady."

"Yeah," I chimed in. "She was radiating hostility, but it's hard to know for sure why. You know? The way Charlie framed it, she's just kinda like that. It's possible that being nasty is how she deals with the heavy stuff."

Sandy nodded thoughtfully. "It would've been nice to talk to some of the others on the ranch. Get some more information about how they go about caring for the horses and what the owners are like when we aren't there. But I didn't see any other employees."

"Yeah, I didn't see anyone, either." After a beat, I added, "I don't know. The owners offing the horses doesn't feel right."

"I noticed cameras in the barn," Sandy added. "I wonder if there are any videos."

"Crap!" I smacked the steering wheel with one hand. "They *do* have cameras in the barn. Mr. Williams was going to save the video from Sunday night and show it to us when we came out. I totally forgot."

"Even if you remembered, I'm not sure they would've shown them to us," Sandy said. "We were definitely not welcome on their property. They just let us out there because they have to keep up appearances."

I glanced quickly at her, trying to read her face before having to turn back to the road. "I'll give him a call when we get back. Maybe he can email me the files."

Sandy snorted, not unkindly. "Let me know if you find anything exciting. I'm not optimistic. I think those two are gonna fight you the whole way through this."

* * *

We pulled into the lab parking lot just before noon, and I couldn't help but feel slightly dejected. We'd gotten one lead—the two types of bait —but otherwise, I didn't have shit to show for a half day poking around the ranch.

"Thanks again, Sandy," I said as we parted ways in the hallway.

"Happy to help. Want me to order the metaldehyde and zinc phosphide tests for you on the stomach contents?"

"Yes, ma'am. That would be great."

"I'll let Lenny and Eva know right now and make sure we get it out in the afternoon pick-up."

We said our goodbyes, and I made it back to my office without another Gerald run-in. The trip to the ranch must have been enough bad juju for one day.

I slumped into my chair and sat looking at the phone for a good five minutes before I choked down my dread. I dialed Adam's number, drawing out the time between poking at the numbers as long as physically possible.

"Hello?" a voice answered.

"Hello, Mr. Williams. It's Dr. Harjo. Thanks for letting us come out today. I realized after we left that we forgot to have a look at the security camera footage. Is it possible to download the files and send them to me?" I spouted everything out without pausing, hoping to get to the meat and potatoes quickly.

There was silence on the other end of the line.

"Mr. Williams? Did I lose you?"

"I'm here. I don't have the footage anymore."

"Huh?" I blurted, assuming I hadn't heard him right.

"The footage gets rewritten every twenty-four hours."

What the hell? I thought.

"Uh, okay. I thought I remembered you saying that you were going to save it. Thanks anyway." I fumbled through my shock. He didn't even sound apologetic or worried.

There was another awkward pause.

He cleared his throat but didn't say anything.

"I'll give you a call when the slides come back, and I can get a look at everything under the microscope." I was scrambling, and he knew it.

He sucked his teeth loud enough for me to catch it.

"Have a nice day, Mr. Williams," I said, at a loss for what to add.

"Goodbye," he said tersely and hung up.

I rested the phone in the cradle, flabbergasted.

Was he just in another stage of grief? Or was he truly angry with me? And why the hell didn't he save the camera footage? I'd specifically asked him to save it. I couldn't help but think that the only reason he would've allowed the footage to be rewritten was if he, or someone else, didn't want anyone to see what was on there.

It wasn't until later, when I was driving back home from work, that I realized how the Williamses might've tipped their hand.

CHAPTER
FIFTEEN

Still feeling off-kilter from the ranch visit, I hid in my office to eat lunch. I needed some space away from the noise to roll everything over in my head.

I was halfway through my salad when my phone dinged. I fished it out of my purse and smiled. It was a text from Armand.

Thinking of you

Still on for lunch tomorrow?

Absolutely!

Looking forward to it

How's work?

Strikes and gutters

!!! You know the big lebowski?

He'd caught the obscure reference; my heart swelled. I scrolled through gifs, trying to find one of The Dude. Selecting one about the rug tying the room together, I hit send.

He replied with a laughing emoji.

How about you?

I'm in Laila's lab this week

Shes great

Yes she is!

Excited to see you

Me too

Hope the rest of your day is better

I sent a smiley emoji before putting my phone back in my purse.

Feeling a bit better after hearing from Armand, I poured through old journal articles on metaldehyde and zinc phosphide poisoning in horses, trying to jog my memory on the lesions that gopher and slug bait toxicity caused.

An hour or so later, a knock on my door startled me from the PubMed rabbit hole. Tom poked his head in my office.

"Are you coming to the lab meeting?" he asked casually.

"Oh, crap! Yeah," I answered, grabbing my iPad and stylus to take notes.

Dr. Tom Lang was another pathologist in the lab. He joined about a year after I did, having trained on the East Coast. We'd both been thrown into the deep end and had held onto each other for dear life to get through those first few years. No matter how good a training program was, there was always a ton of stuff left to learn once we were released into the real world. I was still learning stuff; the Shadowhawk case was a perfect example of that.

"Surprised to see you back early," I said, walking with him to the conference room.

In addition to Tom, a third pathologist, Dr. Zoe Smith, rounded out the team at the lab. Tom and Zoe had been on separate vacations, which was why I'd had back-to-back weeks on the necropsy floor.

"I'm just in for the lab meeting. When I'm gone for more than a week, I always feel out of touch with the routine."

"I hear you," I said. "I had to delete my email off my phone so I'd stop checking it every second when I was on vacation."

He laughed in sympathy. We both struggled to disconnect completely; we cared too much about the animals.

"How was your trip?" I asked as I held the door to the conference room for him.

"It was great. You should get out to the Ozarks sometime. The pictures don't do it justice."

"Glad you had a nice time with no cell reception." I shot him a smile.

We grabbed seats as others started entering the room. I slid into a chair between Dr. Manuel Rodriguez, the head of the virology and serology labs, and Sandy. Gerald was already seated across from me, smirking. The director, Fran Jones, came in last and took the seat at the head of the table.

The director, the head of each of the labs, and the pathologists met every Wednesday afternoon to discuss relevant updates or other important lab-related issues. It was also an opportunity to pick the collective brain about any difficult cases.

"A few quick updates," Fran kicked things off, "EH&S will be out next month for an inspection. Please make sure everything is all set in your labs. Last time, we had some issues with lab coat compliance. Make sure everyone is wearing a lab coat when in the lab and remind people to take their lab coat off before going to the bathroom."

Everyone around the table nodded. The diagnostic lab had been built in the days before personal protective equipment was a thing. People only started wearing gloves about thirty years ago. And, before that, they'd be smoking and eating on the necropsy floor. Because of the layout of the offices, labs, and other rooms, it was really difficult to separate clean and dirty areas. It was also super easy to forget to put your lab coat on or take it off in clean areas like the breakroom.

"Next, the renderer has informed us that they will be stopping service in three months. Until we get the digestor up and running, we'll need to come up with another plan."

"What?!" Tom and I exclaimed at the same time.

All of the small animal carcasses were either sent for private or group cremation off-site. The large animals were sent to the renderer. Without that service, we'd be stacking up bodies in the fridge pretty fast. We'd gotten funding for a large digestor to help with the disposal of the large carcasses. But that was about a year away from being operational.

"Can we rush the install?" I asked.

"Unfortunately, no. The unit isn't even in the country yet," Fran said.

I traded a worried look with Tom. If Dustin didn't already know, he was going to flip a lid when he heard about this.

"This could get really bad, really fast." Tom drummed his fingers on the table, brow furrowed.

"We may have to send them to the landfill," Fran said matter-of-factly.

Tom and I stared at Fran, dumbfounded.

"Is that even legal?" I asked.

"We'll figure it out." Fran waved her hand dismissively. "I'm working with the dean on solutions." Before the panic could get any worse, she changed the subject. "How are things in the labs?"

"Avian influenza testing is picking up," Manuel chimed in. "We received over one thousand samples last week. We're doing our best, but we may need to think about overtime or getting some temp help in."

"Are we seeing anything come through on the floor?" Fran asked.

"Nope. No birds have come in since I've been on. How about you, Tom?" I asked. He'd been on duty before going on vacation.

"No birds." He shrugged. "Most chicken farms don't submit carcasses."

Fran and I nodded. A necropsy on a chicken was cost-prohibitive for most chicken farmers. They almost always ran close to the red line. The flu testing was mandated, though, especially with the outbreak happening up north.

"How about the micro and tox labs?" Fran asked.

"Microbiology is doing well," Gerald said. "We are seeing increased volumes without the need for overtime." He glanced over at Manuel. "Turnaround time is also superlative."

"How 'bout you, Sandy?" Fran said.

"Things are steady in toxicology. We've had a handful of high sulfurs in water. Blue-green algae is starting to peak again. But, other than Josie's case, it's the usual," Sandy reported.

"Is that the case that the police called you about?" Gerald said smugly.

Everyone turned to look at me. To my horror, my cheeks warmed. "Yes, it is. I've got a weird case that I'd like to bounce off everyone if we have time."

"The floor is yours," Fran said, twirling her hand in a "keep going" motion.

"The patient is a thirteen-year-old quarter horse. They've had four horses die in less than a week."

Tom let out a low whistle.

"Yeah, I know. Pretty rough. Other than evidence of thrashing right before death, there are no signs. The horses are vaccinated. And, virology testing was negative."

Manuel nodded. "I saw that case come through. I expected an EHV outbreak based on the history. Was surprised to see it come up negative."

"Me, too," Sandy added.

"I wish it had been herpes so I could be done with this case," I continued, "but the horses were vaccinated, so I wasn't super hopeful. The horses are kept in stalls and fed alfalfa and pelleted feed. They drink city water. They don't have access to pasture. Sandy and I went on a tour of the ranch just this morning. Sandy?"

Sandy jumped in. "With viral disease ruled out, we're thinking a toxicity. The waterers were all functional and clean. The alfalfa was beautiful, with no weeds, toxic plants, or beetles that I could find. The pelleted feed is a little suspicious. We sent it in, just in case."

"Anything on gross?" Tom asked, interested. A pathologist couldn't resist a mystery.

"Squeaky clean," I answered. "I'm hoping to get the histo back on the internal organs today. I won't be able to trim the brain and spinal cord until tomorrow or Friday at the earliest. I'm hoping there's something there."

"Sure you didn't miss anything?" Gerald asked. "When I was at K-state, there was one pathologist who always overlooked things. If it wasn't for my lab, she would've misdiagnosed half her cases." He sat back in his chair, face relaxed and sincere.

Everyone at the table turned to look at him. Tom rolled his eyes. Fran stiffened and pulled her lips into a thin white line.

What the hell, Gerald? Was that a jab or just a socially awkward blurt?

Sandy came to my rescue. "After that completely unhelpful comment…. Any thoughts on differentials?" She directed the question to Tom and Manuel.

The skin around Gerald's eyes tightened.

"I'm with you. It has to be something toxic. You won't know until the histo comes back," Tom said, echoing what I'd been thinking for the last six days.

I just couldn't get those slides back fast enough.

"Maybe you should take over the case now that you're back, Tom. Make sure no other animals die," Gerald said.

"Have any more died?" Fran asked, ignoring Gerald.

I was sure she was cursing the day she hired him as tenured faculty. But my empathy for her position could only go so far; she tolerated his behavior, which was almost as bad as saying those things herself.

"Not since Monday," I answered.

"What's changed?" Manuel asked.

"They stopped feeding the pelleted feed and flushed the watering system. But, other than that, nothing that I'm aware of." I chewed the inside of my cheek. "The owner thinks a disgruntled ranch hand poisoned the horses."

Gerald snorted loudly.

"Yeah, yeah, I know," I said, nervously tapping my stylus on the table. "But something is off about this case. I guess this ranch hand was fired right before the deaths started, and he allegedly assaulted one of the owners on Sunday, right before the latest horse died. That's what the police called about—the assault."

I sighed, looking at the doubtful faces around the table. I felt like a conspiracy theorist, but I couldn't ignore the facts before me.

"Plus, the horses are insured," I continued, "and the owner keeps asking when they'll be paid. I guess the ranch has financial struggles."

"Did you call Adam about the camera footage?" Sandy asked.

"Camera footage?" Manual repeated with a hint of excitement.

"Yeah, they have cameras in the barn," I answered. "We'd planned on taking a look at the footage when we were there today. But it slipped our minds."

Gerald let out an exacerbated huff.

I flashed him a glare and pressed on. "I called him when we got back. They'd erased all of the footage even though I'd asked them to save it."

"Huh," Tom said, crossing his arms and leaning back in his chair.

"'Huh' is right." Sandy picked up the story. "They also buried the other dead horses before we could get a look at them."

I nodded. "They're just acting weird. I don't think we can fully rule out the horses being intentionally poisoned. Since they're kept in stalls with limited access to anything out on pasture, we have to focus on what is being brought into the barn."

"We did find some gopher bait and slug bait in the barn under the sink and away from the feed," Sandy said.

"Is that toxic to horses?" Fran asked.

Sandy nodded. "You might get lucky enough to see a pale liver on gross with zinc phosphide toxicity. But not much else. Josie saved stomach contents. Lenny already packaged it up for testing, and it should go out with the afternoon pick up."

Heads nodded around the table.

"Anything we might be missing?" I looked at Manuel and Tom.

"I don't have any better ideas," Manuel said, shrugging. "I agree that the next step is histo. Sorry."

"Me, neither," Tom chimed in. "I think you're just gonna have to wait for histo, especially the brain."

"That's an unusual case. It may end up getting publicity. We don't want this to get ugly. Keep us posted, especially if the police contact you again," Fran said.

I nodded.

"And don't let any more die," Gerald jabbed with a smirk. The shitass just couldn't help himself.

* * *

Back in my office, I sat at my desk, eyes closed, and took a few deep breaths. Gerald was an expert at pushing my buttons.

Just as I was about to run away into my emails, there was a light knock at the door.

"Come in," I called out.

"I have slides for you," Noah said, handing me a couple of flats.

I felt my stomach tighten.

"Thank you," I said, placing the flats on my desk.

Noah left quietly, shutting the door behind him.

Unable to resist, I flipped back the cardboard cover. Sure enough, they were the slides from the Shadowhawk case. I slid the first one onto the microscope. Slide after slide skated across the stage as I scrambled to find any clue as to what was killing the horses.

With a sigh, I leaned back. All the internal organ sections were within normal limits. My heart sank as I realized I would need to type up yet another report that said fuck-all. Days like this made me feel like a charlatan, especially with Gerald poking at me.

Negative results are just as important as positive ones, I reminded myself.

There was some truth to that. The liver was normal, which made gopher bait unlikely. Poisoning with zinc phosphide in gopher bait was associated with fat accumulation in the liver, which I hadn't seen grossly and confirmed was absent microscopically. I'd have to check with Sandy, though. I wasn't sure if a high enough dose could kill a horse without any microscopic changes in the liver. A normal liver also ruled out several other toxins.

To rule out slug bait, I'd have to wait for the brain and spinal cord sections, and those were a long way off. They hadn't even fixed enough to trim. I'd just have to try to be patient and hope that everything would eventually come together.

Despite the internal attempts at cheer, I still knew the situation sucked, and the owners would be pissed. I felt hopeless, and, worst of all, more horses might die. As I was wallowing in self-pity, the phone rang.

"Dr. Harjo. How can I help you?"

"Hello, Doc," Carol said. "I have Officer Watts on the line for you.

I bit my tongue so the "fucking seriously?" wouldn't slip out.

In the pause, Carol continued, "Would you like to take it, or should I send him to voicemail?"

"Send him through, thanks." I felt bile in the back of my throat. Better to face this shit now than kick the can down the road.

After two clicks, Carol said, "Officer Watts. I have Dr. Harjo for you. Have a nice day." She clicked off before either of us could reply.

"Hello, Officer Watts. This is Dr. Harjo. How can I help you?"

"Hello, Dr. Harjo. Sorry to bother you again. This is about JW Ranch."

"Yes, sir. The Shadowhawk case. How can I help?" I asked, feeling dread creep up my spine.

"As a reminder, we have an alleged assault that occurred with a disgruntled employee on Sunday. We questioned the employee yesterday." He cleared his throat. "He was quite agitated and under the influence when we spoke to him. He had knowledge of the dead horses on the ranch and that one was brought to your facility for an autopsy."

I didn't have the guts to correct him when he said "autopsy." Instead, I sat there meekly, wondering how the hell I'd gotten into this mess.

He cleared his throat again. "Anyway, I can't share much more. But he did make verbal threats against you."

My heart fell into my shoes.

"I'd ask that you please be extra cautious. He's a white male, about 6'2, with short brown hair and blue eyes. If you see anything suspicious or feel unsafe, please call 911." He paused.

I was gobsmacked and couldn't formulate anything more than an "Uh...."

"Dr. Harjo?"

"Yes," I said, blood finally returning to my brain so I could sound half-intelligent again. "Sorry. I'm just surprised. This doesn't happen often...or at all, really...in my world. So...I'm just a bit...," I rambled.

"I understand," he said in a tone that lacked any hint of empathy. "Please stay safe and be aware of your surroundings."

"Yes, sir," was all I could say.

"Again, if you find anything in the horse, please let me know. Do you have my number?"

"Yes, sir. It's on my desk," I answered.

After polite goodbyes, I rested the phone in the cradle.

With my heart still thudding in my chest, I slumped back in my chair. Today had been one giant shitshow, and I sensed a pint of ice cream in my future.

CHAPTER
SIXTEEN

When I arrived at work on Thursday, I had two bodies waiting for me. Since neither of them was from JW Ranch, I was eager to jump in and get lost in the rhythm of a different case.

Dustin was already out on the necropsy floor. A dead steer was laid out on the hydraulic table, and a cat was on one of the smaller, free-standing tables. With a large animal on the docket for this morning, I'd donned coveralls and rubber boots.

Dustin turned down the music when he saw me sloshing through the footbaths. "Mornin', Dr. Harjo."

"Morning. What've we got?" I asked, grabbing my knife to put a quick edge on it.

"Both of 'em are sudden death," he answered.

I quickly read through the paperwork. The steer had been found dead at a feedlot and had (fortunately) been brought in right away. It looked relatively fresh, and I thanked my lucky stars it wasn't a stinker; I had my lunch with Armand today.

The kicker was, with the limited history, I was going to have to rule out anthrax before we started digging in, especially since there was blood dripping from its nose. That meant a delay in getting started. On the upside, we ran the anthrax test in-house, and it wouldn't take as long as a rabies test.

"Let's collect some blood from the steer and send it over to microbiology to rule out anthrax just to be safe," I said. "I'll get started on the cat while we wait."

"On it." Dustin nodded and went about collecting blood, filling out the paperwork, and busing the sample to the lab.

Only certified staff were allowed to call a blood sample positive or negative for anthrax. If this steer had come in on the weekend, we'd be paging someone in, which could take hours. But Gerald was certified, and I'd dodged him in the hallway, so I knew he was in today. We should have results back from a direct smear of the blood within the hour.

I traded my knife out for a scalpel and headed over to the cat. The cat's history was equally unhelpful. The patient was a seven-year-old, domestic short-haired cat. The owners had reported that the cat was lethargic the day before, and they found it dead outside this morning. The owners were worried that the neighbor had poisoned it.

I couldn't help but roll my eyes. People had zero trust in anybody else anymore. It was more likely that the cat had been hit by a car or died from hypertrophic cardiomyopathy.

On external examination, everything looked in order. There was no evidence of frayed claws or skin abrasions that I would expect to see with a hit-by-car case. I quickly opened the body cavities and did a quick once-over of the abdomen and chest. There was no evidence of bleeding or bruising to suggest trauma, and I was confident ruling that out.

Just as I started removing the internal organs, Dustin was back and assisting.

"See anything yet?" he asked.

"Doesn't look like trauma."

When I pulled back the stomach to remove the GI tract, I froze. The spleen was extremely large and speckled with dozens of white dots.

"Shit!" I hissed, stepping back.

Dustin, knowing what I was thinking, went to the supply cabinets and pulled out N95 masks and disposable arm covers. I put the scalpel down and pulled off my dirty gloves, dropping them in the biohazard bag. I put the mask and arm covers on before donning a fresh set of gloves and getting back to it.

The changes within the spleen were non-specific and could be caused by half a dozen things. But—and it was an important "but"—one of those things was tularemia. The disease was common enough to be of concern in Oklahoma, and people could get it. Smart people didn't mess around with tularemia; it was highly infectious, and mortality rates could reach sixty percent if untreated.

With additional protective equipment donned, I continued the necropsy. I pressed sections of the spleen on a microscope slide to make an impression smear. I set it aside to air-dry before staining it. The slides would help me rule in/out one of my other differentials: a systemic yeast infection caused by *Histoplasma* spp.

I saved fresh spleen in Petri dishes, should I need them later for microbiology or PCR testing. With samples from all of the abdominal organs sinking in the formalin container, I moved to the chest. Based on the spleen, I didn't think the cat had hypertrophic cardiomyopathy, but I still needed to take a closer look at the heart.

Upon removal of the pluck, the thyroid glands looked normal. I tossed them in the formalin container for safekeeping. I then weighed the heart and took measurements of the chamber thickness, the inner circumference of the chambers, and the inner circumference of the aorta and vena cava. Though the heart visually looked normal, all of the data I collected confirmed that the heart wasn't enlarged.

"Want me to Diff-Quik the slide for you?" Dustin asked, gesturing to the impression smear of the spleen.

"Sure, thanks."

As the slide dried, Dustin bagged the cat's remains, and I jotted down my necropsy notes. Working together, we scrubbed down the table and tools using extra sanitizer. The smell burned my nose even through the N95 mask.

By the time we'd finished tidying up, the slide was dry. I tossed it on the stage of the rickety microscope we kept on the necropsy floor. It was older than I was, but I could still see well enough to spot some of the larger organisms. To my relief, dozens of yeast organisms mixed with blood filled the slide.

Pulling my mask down over my chin, I called out, "It's histoplasmosis. Just store all of the samples. I'll issue the gross report and offer PCR to confirm. But I suspect they'll want to save some money and pass on any additional testing."

Dustin responded with a thumbs up as he moved the hose around the steer, eager to get started on the next case. Despite his antsiness, we'd still have to wait until we heard from the microbiology lab.

Veterinary pathologists always had to be cautious with zoonotic diseases. Thankfully, we didn't accept primates at the lab, which posed the biggest risk. We wore lab coats and gloves, which protected us from 99% of diseases we could get from non-primate species. But there were some nasty diseases we just didn't mess with that could make a star appearance in a non-primate species, like rabies, anthrax, and tularemia.

Having two suspect cases on the same day pretty much sucked and was just proof that I had the luck of a gremlin. I was hoping I was soaking up my fair share of bad karma this morning to have an awesome lunch with Armand later. Thinking of him, my stomach fluttered.

The sound of the necropsy door thudding closed shook me out of my daydream. Gerald stomped over, chasing away the flitter of positive thoughts.

"Hey, man. I've told you this before," Dustin called out, angry, "you gotta wear boots and a coat out here." He pointed back out the door to redirect Gerald off the necropsy floor.

Gerald rolled his eyes but complied. I couldn't help but wonder if he would have acquiesced so easily if *I* had been the one asking. He still stepped over the footbath without dipping his shoes, the little turd.

Dustin turned to me, shaking his head and throwing his hands up in the air.

You and me both, I thought, flashing him a knowing look.

Gerald returned a minute later, wearing a lab coat and shoe covers. "Have you figured out the horse case yet?"

Dustin and I exchanged a glance. We were standing here next to an anthrax suspect, and he came out to throw a punch.

I sighed. "We don't know much more than what I shared yesterday."

"The histology lab said they gave you the slides. Have you bothered to look at them yet? There are other horses at risk on the ranch. They can't wait for people to be faffing about," Gerald prodded.

Seriously? Why is he shopping for things to throw in my face?

Dustin cleared his throat as he leaned back on the counter, hands in his coveralls. It was as close to a warning as Gerald was going to get.

"Yes. The slides came back on the internal organs yesterday. Unfortunately, there were no significant histologic changes," I said, trying to keep my voice neutral.

"How many sections of the liver did you look at? Zinc phosphide causes hepatic vacuoles. Did you look for those?" he pressed.

"Yes, Gerald. Believe it or not, I'm board-certified in anatomic pathology, and I've been doing this for a long time." An annoyed sigh escaped despite my best efforts.

Changing tact, he crossed his arms and said, "Clearly, the horses have been poisoned. If Sandy could do her job, the owners would have an answer now."

Out of the corner of my eye, I saw Dustin stiffen.

"Sandy's on top of it," I said, hating myself for feeling like I had to defend the best veterinary toxicologist in the world to a mediocre microbiologist.

"Was there a reason you came out here?" Dustin asked brusquely, stepping forward.

"Oh, yes," Gerald said, eyebrows lifting over wide eyes. "My technicians rushed the sample, and I wanted to inform you that the steer is negative for anthrax."

"Thank you," I said, trying to be polite, and turned to Dustin. "We can go ahead and get started, then."

As if I hadn't just spoken, Gerald chimed, "Since it's negative, you're clear to do the necropsy."

"Thank you, Dr. Richter. *You're* free to go so that we can get started," Dustin said, unable to hide his irritation.

Gerald smirked and stayed put. Looking at me, he said, "I don't know why you always get your panties in a bunch. We never see anthrax."

Adrenaline rushed through me, and I fought the urge to laugh in his face. In the diagnostic lab, we saw one or two anthrax cases a year. It would be Dustin and one of the pathologists risking their biscuits out on the necropsy floor if the animal had died from anthrax. By the time it got to the lab, the sample was all neat and tidy and could be worked in a fume hood, where everyone was safe. Gerald didn't have a clue.

Ignoring the comment, I said, "Thank you for the verbal results. You should go so that you don't get blood or rumen contents on you."

His grin dropped, and he squinted his eyes slightly. He then turned, dropping his boot covers on the floor by the footbath instead of in the trash on his way out.

As soon as the door closed behind him, Dustin said, "Fran has to do something about him. He can't act like that." He turned toward me, concerned. "You okay?"

"Yeah, it's just Gerald being Gerald. I've gotten used to it."

"Doesn't make it right," Dustin grumbled. "And y'all shouldn't have to 'get used to it.' You know?"

"Yeah, I know." I shrugged. "But what can I do about it? All of us have complained to Fran a dozen times. Because he's tenured, she just says her hands are tied."

"The behavior shouldn't be tolerated just because you think that no one will take action. Y'all have rights," Dustin pressed gently.

I grabbed my knife and held up the front leg of the steer. Dustin grabbed the leg, helping me reflect it. We went through the usual motions of opening the carcass as we talked.

"You're right. I know you are. It's just hard. I haven't lost hope that Fran will step in, but I always get nervous about escalating concerns. I've got my own tenure review coming up in a year."

"That's illegal, them passing you up for tenure because you filed a complaint," Dustin said firmly.

"I know, but they won't say it's because of that. They'll make up some excuse. Sandy has told some horror stories."

We finished opening up the cavities, and the rumen popped up like a balloon. Dustin thumped on it and laughed.

"Bet you five bucks it's bloat," he said.

"No way. I'm not betting to lose. It's totally bloat." I grinned back at him. I grabbed the loppers and started to take the chest cavity off.

"Want me to go to HR?" Dustin asked, not letting the subject drop. "I don't want to step on your toes. But I got your back. Whatever you need." There was genuine concern in his voice.

It felt good to know that he supported me. There were a lot of great people in the lab, and we couldn't let one rotten apple ruin the bunch.

"If I'm going to escalate it to HR, I'll do it myself."

"Document everything," Dustin advised.

"I have been." I shrugged. "But I just keep hoping Fran will do something."

We dug out the gastrointestinal tract, and it slid to the floor with a *slurp*. Eager to test out our theory, I opened the rumen. It was almost three times the normal size and filled with frothy, bright green, partially digested feed.

As I was working on that, Dustin pulled out the pluck. He slid his knife down the esophagus, reflecting it open. Sure enough, there was a beautiful bloat line at the level of the thoracic inlet, with the proximal portion bright red and the distal portion blanched white.

"Ding, ding, ding," Dustin said. "We've got a frothy bloat."

We knuckle-bumped our bloody gloves.

"It's nice to get an easy case every once in a while," I said.

I checked all of the organs to make sure there wasn't a twofer before we dumped everything in the offal bins.

As we were slopping them in, Dustin asked, "Want to save any samples?"

"Naw. I'm confident in this one."

We finished up in companionable silence, tossing the last bits and bobs into the offal bin. As Dustin operated the hoist to move the carcass into the fridge, I hosed down the table.

The large fridge doors closed with a loud *bang*, and he came back out to help me finish up.

He was a keeper; he worked hard and did his job well. On top of that, he treated people fairly and with respect.

My heart swelling with appreciation for my coworker and friend, I said, "Hey, Dustin. Thanks for being there. I appreciate the support."

He held his hand up, and we fist-bumped again.

"Any time, Doc."

* * *

Back in my office in my civvies, I took a deep whiff of my hair. All I could smell was the faint traces of my shampoo. I felt my shoulders relax. Even though the steer had been fresh, the smell of rumen contents still had a way of sticking.

As soon as I opened the first case to type up the report, the phone rang.

"Dr. Harjo. How can I help you?" I answered.

"Hello, Dr. Harjo," Carol replied. "I have a gentleman on the line for you. It's a Josh Jones."

My eyebrows furrowed. "Did he give an accession number?"

Carol rattled the number off. "Would you like me to transfer the call or send him to voicemail?"

"Go ahead and send him through."

I quickly looked up the accession as Carol made the introductions. My heart sank as soon as the case opened.

"Dr. Harjo?" a masculine voice asked, shaking me out of my silence.

"Yes, sir. This is Dr. Harjo. To whom am I speaking?"

"This is Josh Jones." His voice was pleasant and upbeat. "I'm a rep from Best in Class feed. Do you have a moment?"

I felt like I was on the precipice of a slippery slope. "Yes," I said hesitantly.

"I'd like to ask you a question about a case," he said in a congenial way and then rattled off the same accession number that Carol had given me.

By that point, I had my shit together and a reply in hand. "Due to privacy laws, I'm unable to discuss this case with you without permission from Mr. Williams."

"Oh!" he said, sounding surprised and slightly embarrassed. "I apologize, ma'am. I wasn't aware that there were privacy laws with animals."

My eyes narrowed at the faint whiff of bullshit. He worked for a feed company; he'd have to be a newbie not to know that, and a newbie wouldn't be put in charge of calling me. I sat in silence, waiting for his next move.

He tried again. "Mr. Williams gave me the accession number and said I could speak with you."

As if I haven't heard that before.

"If Mr. Williams would like me to share information about the case with you, he'll need to call me directly to provide verbal permission," I said, holding my ground.

"Oh, okay. We replaced the feed out there. We were wondering why Mr. Williams was concerned about it." His voice was still friendly, but I couldn't help hearing the warning bells.

"Mr. Williams can share that information with you directly, or he can call me to give me permission to speak with you." I was starting to wish this call had gone to voicemail.

"I understand," he acquiesced. "I'll call Mr. Williams right after this. In the meantime, can you answer some general questions about feed?"

Nice try, buddy.

I'd encountered this tactic before. Pretty soon, he'd start asking general questions, like if such-and-such could cause a death, how an animal might get infected, or how an animal might have access to a toxin. No way in hell was I going on the record one way or another regarding this case. Everyone involved could wait for my final report.

"We'll have to connect another day," I replied. "I'm pretty busy and need to get some reports out."

"Oh, okay. I'll leave my number," he said, unable to hide his disappointment. He provided his phone number, which I wrote down in case he asked me to read it back. But I had no intention of calling him unless Mr. Williams asked me to

We exchanged terse goodbyes, and I hung up.

I knew some people might think I was being a bit rude, but pathologists had to be careful who they shared case information with. We couldn't speak to company reps, like from a vaccine or feed company, unless we had permission from the submitter. These cases could get pretty hairy once people started pointing fingers.

Frustrated to have even more drama complicating the Shadowhawk case, I dove into writing the reports for the cases from this morning, eager to finish them before my lunch with Armand.

CHAPTER
SEVENTEEN

I had just enough time to get the gross reports from the steer and the cat released before I had to dash out the door for my date with Armand.

Getting into the car, I took another deep sniff—a last-minute check. Thankfully, both carcasses had been fresh, and I'd escaped stank-free. Sure, I'd gotten blood from the steer all over my arms and splashed on my face. But that was easy enough to wash off.

Red Rock was packed, but I managed to grab a parking spot out front. My heart lurched when I caught sight of Armand. Despite the heat, he was waiting outside for me. He was wearing a slightly fitted, short-sleeve polo, khakis, and dress sneakers. He looked fantastic, and I couldn't help fussing with my hair.

As soon as I stepped out of the car, I caught his eye, and a huge smile spread across his face. He walked over and gave me a light hug.

"Thanks for coming to lunch. It's great to see you," he said, smiling.

"Thanks for inviting me." I pushed my hair back behind my ears for the millionth time, unable to stop the nervous fiddling.

Geez, I wasn't usually this goofy. He was going to think I was a dork.

He held the door for me and then followed me in.

"Are you okay?" he asked with concern.

"Huh?" I said, worried that my obsessive fidgeting might be creeping him out.

He looked at me with eyebrows creased and pointed to my right elbow. "There's blood on the back of your arm. Are you okay?"

I twisted my arm to examine the back of it. Mortified, I realized there was a palm-sized swath of caked blood just below the sleeve of my dress.

"Uh…yeah, I'm fine," I sputtered. "Excuse me for a sec."

As I fled to the bathroom, I noticed a flash of confusion cross his face. I flipped the lock of the bathroom door and turned toward the mirror, peering over my shoulder at the back of my upper arm. I sighed.

Of course, I had to miss a spot today of all days.

I washed the dried steer blood off the back of my arm, trying not to get water on my clothes. The paper towel dispenser was frustratingly stingy, and it took four or five goes to get enough to dry my arm off. After triple-checking myself in the mirror to make sure I hadn't missed anything else, I went back out front.

"Is everything all right?" he asked with genuine concern.

"I'm fine, thank you. I…."

I toyed with the idea of concocting a wild explanation. I decided honesty was the best policy and pressed forward, hoping I wouldn't ruin another date with my air of death.

"I had blood on my arm from a necropsy this morning." I shrugged, trying to hide my embarrassment.

He was unfazed and asked, "Does that happen often?" His lips curled in a slight smile.

"Oh, God, no. But some of the real messy ones can be hard to clean up after without a shower. Even then, I've picked bone flecks out of my hair sometimes. I'd take blood over rumen contents any time. That stuff is nasty, and the smell sticks." I noticed my rambling and stopped short.

Good lord, Josie. Shut up already. I might as well hand him a shovel so he could help me dig a deeper hole.

174

To my immense surprise, he flashed me a grin. "All in a day's work, I guess. You should get hazard pay for that."

I blurted out a laugh and felt my shoulders relax.

"Let's order," he said.

And with that, the moment passed without the slightest feeling of humiliation.

The place was busy but not too noisy, and we made our way through the queue quickly. We ordered at the counter; he got the broccoli chowder soup even though it was flaming hot outside, and I ordered the apple chicken salad sandwich on walnut bread. When it came time to pay, I pulled out my wallet.

Before I could pull cash out, he said, "I got this. You can grab the next one."

He paid for the meal with his card and then stuffed a hefty cash tip into the tip jar.

It was the absolute perfect thing to say to me, and I couldn't help but smile. Not only had he treated me like an equal, but he also promised to see me again. To top it off, he'd provided a generous tip. And, most important of all, he didn't mind me bringing a bit of work on our date. This guy was pretty awesome.

He took our order number, and we grabbed the last open table. "How was work today? Other than getting blood everywhere?"

"Pretty good. Two easy cases. I like the ones where I can issue the report the same day and get the results out."

"Are most of them like that?"

"Eh." I held my hand up and made a so-so motion. "Most times. I have a good idea of what the cause of death is before I leave the floor. I might need a test or two to confirm my suspicion, but I get enough to issue a helpful gross report. The rest of them, I need histo before I know for sure."

"Histo?"

"Oh, sorry. Histology. Looking at the tissues under the microscope."

He nodded in understanding. "Are you always able to determine the cause of death?"

"Most of the time, yes. It might take extra testing, but we usually get an answer. It's pretty rare when we exhaust everything and still don't know what happened. Usually, that's when the carcasses are too rotten to do anything with them."

Or when someone uses a random poison to kill a bunch of horses, and there are zero lesions.

After a pause, I added, "Those days can be rough."

"I find pathology fascinating. You're like a detective." His eyes lit up.

"Kinda, I guess." I shrugged one shoulder shyly, secretly thinking his interest was awesome. "I enjoy it because every case is a puzzle. When I get an animal with no history, it could literally be *anything*: cancer, infectious disease, toxin ingestion…any of those. The best part is when I can help an owner feel a bit better or help the rest of the animals in a herd. Those days, pathologists feel like rock stars." I grinned.

"That's so cool. So, what's the most interesting case you've ever had?"

"Oh…." I pursed my lips. "That's a hard one."

Most of the cases that stuck in my head were the depressing ones. I hated thinking about those, and I certainly didn't want to ruin the mood by sharing them over lunch.

"The infectious disease outbreaks are the most interesting to me, especially ones that result in fetal death or stillbirths. The placenta is such a beautiful organ. And when I can help the rest of the herd or flock to prevent further deaths, that's a win.

"But," I continued, "the weirdest case I've heard of is probably the one that's been passed down by generations of residents." I grinned, remembering it. "We had this giant bowling ball on a shelf in the residents' office with a little plaque from like the 50s or 60s, saying it was from the stomach of an alligator at a zoo."

Armand's eyebrows went up. "They pulled a bowling bowl out of an alligator?" he asked, incredulous.

"Yep." I nodded. "And rumor has it that the alligator's keeper used to bowl and would bring his ball to work with him so he could bowl on the way home."

"Noooo!" he exclaimed in shock.

"Yes," I answered, leaning over the table. "So, the keeper disappeared after work one night. Then, about five or ten years later, the alligator died of 'natural causes.' It came in for a necropsy, and they found a bowling ball in the stomach. One can only assume what happened to the keeper." I leaned back and shrugged, feigning innocence.

"Wow," he said, shaking his head. "Is that a true story?"

I laughed. "The bowling ball is there in the office, and it was definitely from the alligator's stomach. Who knows about the rest."

He grinned. "That's a good one."

A waiter came and swapped our number for our food, and we both dug in.

"How's your visit so far?" I asked between bites.

"It's been wonderful. Laila is a great host. I rotated through one lab last week. I'm in her lab this week and next. They're lucky here. The campus has a lot of equipment, resources, and grad students."

The conversation drifted to his work, and we talked about plant genes as we ate. Time sped by as we laughed and joked. I felt perfectly comfortable with him and soon forgot about the crap waiting back for me at work.

"Do you miss home?" I asked.

"Laila set me up in a pretty nice short-term rental. So, I don't miss my place much, but I do miss my dog, Ileana. It was hard leaving her with my brother for these few months. I know he'll take care of her, but I miss her a lot."

My chest tightened. *Could this guy be any more awesome?*

"What kind of dog is she?" I asked.

He pulled out his phone and showed me a few pictures. She was a medium-sized mutt. In every picture, she had a huge dog grin, tongue hanging out. I loved the fact that he showed off her pictures. Men who showed off pics of their pets usually had soft hearts.

"How about you? Any pets?" he asked, slipping his phone back into his pocket.

"I have a cat. His name's Yersi. He's a little sassy pants."

I whipped out my phone to show him pics.

"Wait," he said. "You have an all-black cat named Yersi?"

"Yes…?" I replied, looking him in the eye, unsure of where he was going.

"Like in *Yersinia pestis*?" He burst out laughing.

Gobsmacked that he caught it, I felt a goofy grin spread across my face. "Yes."

"Like the Black Death." He grinned. "That's clever."

Yeah, he's a keeper.

"Why the 'death' part? Does he hunt a lot?" he asked.

"Yeah, he slays canned food with the best of 'em."

We both snickered.

"He's indoor only. But, if you asked him, I'm sure he'd say that 'The Black Death' is the perfect name. He thinks very highly of himself."

We continued talking companionably as the restaurant emptied and the background noise died down. Realizing that it was almost 2 P.M., I reluctantly started packing up.

"I've got to get back. I'm on duty." I paused and smiled at him. "I enjoyed lunch. Thank you."

"Let me get that," he said, grabbing the dishes to bus to the front.

He walked me to my car with his hand on my back. It was a soft, familiar touch and felt just right.

I turned to him to say goodbye, hoping he would kiss me. Instead, he gently reached out to squeeze my hand and said, "I had a wonderful time. I'd love to see you again."

"Me, too," I said, surprised to feel my cheeks flush.

His eyes searched my face. "May I kiss you?" he asked.

"Oh, absolutely." I grinned mischievously and leaned in.

And, good lord, was he a great kisser—soft and delicate.

He pulled back. His voice husky, he asked, "Are you free at all this weekend?"

"Yes," I practically whispered, trying to catch my breath. "How about dinner on Saturday?"

He smiled and took a step back, still holding my fingers lightly.

"I can cook for you at my place if you'd like. You can meet Yersi."

"Sounds wonderful." He gave my hand a light squeeze and flashed me a sweet smile before heading to his car.

* * *

Still floating on cloud nine after the wonderful lunch with Armand, I put some good tunes on and walked to the histology lab. There was a chance that the brain and spinal cord from the Shadowhawk case would be ready to trim. For a large horse brain, I was pushing my luck; it hadn't even been a week yet. But I was feeling lucky.

I grabbed a lab coat and looped my hair into a bun around a pen. The techs were busy at the cutting benches. We exchanged a wave as I dug a fresh pair of gloves from the box on the wall, then sorted through the buckets and found the brain and spinal cord.

Taking the buckets to a fume hood, I popped each one open. The brain was resting at the bottom and had a tan tinge. The spinal cord was floating in loose, off-white loops.

I fished the brain out of the bucket and rested it on the cutting board. It was still slightly soft, which was not a good sign. I decided to risk a cut to see how fixed it was. My old neurology professor would be rolling in their grave seeing me trim it now. But sometimes, exceptions had to be made for the greater good of the herd.

I made a small cut with the brain knife. About two millimeters in, the brain was bright pink to red.

Crap. It's still raw.

I liked to toe the line when it came to fixation. But there was no way I could trim this brain without making a mess of it. Disappointed, I gently placed the brain back in the bucket and put both buckets back on the cart. Monday would be the earliest I could check on them again. This damn case was going to hang over me for *another* weekend.

My mind was caught in an anxiety loop as I fretted over the Shadowhawk case. I was so distracted on my way back to my office that I walked right into Gerlad's ambush. I stopped short, about a foot away from him, as he angled his body to pin me against the wall and block my escape.

"There you are. I've been looking for you." He leaned one arm against the wall.

I looked up at him, resisting the urge to step back, and crossed my arms. "Yes? What do you need?"

"You're beautiful. You should work less, find a husband, and settle down," he admonished.

"Good lord, Gerald." I sighed as my frustration bubbled over. "Don't you ever quit? That isn't appropriate to say. Do you have anything work-related to talk about?"

He dropped his arm and forced his hands into his pockets. "No. You're just so wrapped up in your work, I want to make sure that you take care of yourself."

I held my hand up in his face. "Thank you, Mr. 1950s. I'll pass."

Sick of his shit, I pushed past him, shaking my head.

Gerald was literally a walking sexual harassment poster. When people take those courses, they always laugh, saying, "Who would ever do that?" Whelp, Gerald would. Like *every day*. And my boss did *nothing*.

In the sanctuary of my office, I collapsed in my chair. Today had been a rollercoaster. The cases this morning were slam dunks, and those small victories always felt good. Further, I had a wonderful lunch with Armand.

Armand….

But then I had the lingering stress of the Shadowhawk case and Gerald stalking the hallway like a big fat turd on what would have been a great day.

As if the universe heard me, my cell binged with a text. I pulled my phone out, reminding myself that it was probably from someone cool and not work-related. Sure enough, it was from Armand.

I had a really nice time today

Me too

Looking forward to seeing you Saturday. Can I bring anything?

No need to bring anything just yourself

Do you have any food preferences?

Nope I'll eat anything

I flushed, my mind going where it shouldn't. Aunty always said my brain lived in the gutter. The phone binged again and shook me out of my daydream.

Thanks for asking

The week can't go by fast enough!

I thumbs-upped the last message and then sent him my address. I would need to think about what to cook. I could shop Saturday morning, maybe harvest some stuff from the garden, and make him something wonderful. I felt my cheeks get warm again.

CHAPTER
EIGHTEEN

To my delight, Friday passed in a bland stream of busy work interrupted by a splash of sparkle. The best part of it was that I didn't have any necropsies. After two back-to-back weeks with a tough case hanging around my neck, I was eager for a Fri-YAY.

The morning sped by quickly as I worked my way through slides from older cases. Lunchtime rolled in, and I grabbed my purse to head out to meet Laila.

As usual, McAlister's was busy with the lunch crowd. Laila stepped away from the counter with her number in hand just as I got in line. I gave her a wave as she went to grab a seat for us. About fifteen minutes later, I wove through the bustling dining area with my water and food order number.

"Hey. How's it going?" I asked as I slid into the booth.

"Pretty good! You?"

A waiter came by and swapped out a sandwich and chips for her number. She grabbed a chip and pushed the plate over to share.

I held my hand up. "I'm good. I can wait."

She pulled the plate back toward her.

"Things have been meh." I shrugged it off and took a sip of water. Laila watched me, one eyebrow raised.

I waved my hand to brush away any negative vibes. "I want to hear about what's going on with you. How's the application for Chair going?"

"Turned it in," she said excitedly.

"Congrats! When will you find out if you got it?" I was thrilled she'd thrown her hat in the ring.

"The application deadline is at the end of the month. Then, they'll select people for interviews. I probably won't know for sure until the start of the school year."

"You're a slam-dunk." I beamed at her.

"Thanks for encouraging me to apply. Ian is pissed, but everyone else is super supportive. And…it just feels good…like I'm doing the right thing." She looked down, bashful.

"You're gonna be awesome in that role. I'm excited for you." I reached over and grabbed her hand.

Her smile radiated happiness, reaching to crinkle the skin around her eyes.

"I have some ideas to help the more junior faculty and grad students with grant writing," she said, going into planning mode. "I'm thinking we should have quarterly workshops. And we should post the upcoming grants and due dates in the main office. I was also thinking we need a social media presence. We can use that to promote what we're doing, and it may help with donors."

Laila continued talking through all of her ideas between chips. She was bursting with energy over her developing strategy. I was proud of her. I was also a bit jealous that she wasn't my boss. She was going to make a great leader.

Out of the blue, she switched topics and asked, "Sooo…how did lunch go with Armand? He's super nice, right? He was in my lab this week, and everyone raved about him."

My stomach flopped just thinking about him. I looked down at the table and fidgeted with a napkin. I felt a smile spread across my face as I searched for the right words.

"Ohhh…. Jooosssiiieee. That good, huh?" she asked mischievously. "Tell me!"

We were interrupted as a waiter set down my Rueben sandwich and potato salad.

"He's great," I said shyly. I put my napkin on my lap.

"Tell me everything!" Laila prodded.

"It didn't start off too hot. I'd just come off the floor and missed some blood on my arm."

"Ew...Josie!" Laila was flabbergasted. "You need to stop going straight from a dead animal to a date!"

"It's my job. I see you with dirt on you all the time. What's the difference?" I said, teasing her.

"It's not *blood*," Laila responded, not unkindly.

I made a mock innocent face and smiled. "It was just blood from a steer with bloat. That's not much further from this." I titled my sandwich to her.

She smirked. "What did Armand do when he saw it?"

"Well, I think he thought it was my blood at first. He asked if I was okay."

"Aww." She clasped her hands dramatically. "That is super cute."

"Yeah, it kinda was. Anyway, I explained. And he didn't care. Like *at all*." I took a bite of my sandwich, enjoying the burst of the sauerkraut and the sharpness of the rye. The Ruebens at McAlister's were the best. "He's really great, Laila. He's interesting, educated, and kind. He also got Yersi's name like that...." I snapped my fingers. "I didn't even have to explain it to him."

Laila's eyebrows went up, and she grinned.

"Yeah, right? And he even thought Yersi's name was cool. I'm having him over for dinner on Saturday." I shrugged and poked my potato salad with my fork. "I'm trying not to get my hopes up too much. I'm also trying to forget that he's just here on sabbatical."

"Three months is a long time," Laila said with a half-smile. "A lot can happen between now and then. You never know."

I nodded, mouth full.

"How's work? How's that horse case you were talking about at dinner last week?" she asked.

"Still no answer." A sigh slipped out. "I think it's something toxic.

But until I get the histo on the brain and spinal cord back, I won't know what rabbit hole to go down next."

"That takes a lot of time, right?"

I nodded. "CNS tissue has to fix in formalin a lot longer than other tissues. I haven't even trimmed it yet."

"Maybe you can trim it today?" she offered hopefully.

"Doubtful. It was still pink yesterday."

She stuck her tongue out, making a gagging face. "I'm eating," she teased.

After a beat, I added, "It's funny. I was dreading going to work this week. I normally love the tough cases; they get my brain working again. This one is different."

Her brows crinkled in genuine concern.

"Ever since the fourth one died on Monday, I worry about finding my voicemail light blinking with reports of more dead horses."

Laila reached over and squeezed my arm. "Maybe they're through the thick of it? Maybe it's just a matter of paperwork and closure now?"

"I hope so," I said, the potato salad leaving a bitter taste in my mouth.

* * *

I woke up Saturday morning way more nervous than I should've been. I was giddy with excitement but also terrified that I would royally screw up the date. Armand felt too good to be true, and I was waiting for the other shoe to drop.

The morning was spent making the house presentable and running to the grocery store. I'd decided to pull out all of the stops and make a Mexican meal from scratch. The meal plan included carnitas, refried beans, and Mexican rice with guacamole. Freshly harvested tomatoes, cilantro, and fresh peppers were chopped into a tasty salsa.

I pretty much sucked at making Mexican desserts. Instead, I made lime bars with fresh limes from the garden. The crust was made from pecans, shredded coconut, and dates, which was always a big hit with most guests.

With the carnitas in the oven to crisp up, I dug through my closet, trying to decide what to wear. I was cooking for him at home, but it was still a date. I wanted him to know that I had put effort into getting ready without being overdressed. I selected one of my favorite casual dresses and a turquoise necklace. I left my hair loose, liking the way it brushed against my bare arms.

Yersi sat in the door of the bathroom, watching me, tail swishing.

"What?"

Meow.

He got up and started slowly weaving around my legs.

"Is that so?"

Meow.

I reached down and scratched his head. He leaned into it, starting to purr. Then, he perked up and scampered out the door. Two seconds later, the doorbell rang. My heart flopped, and I couldn't wipe away the goofy grin. I opened the door, and Armand smiled gently.

My chest tightened again when I saw him. His dark hair was wavy and unstyled. He wore a casual, button-up shirt that stretched over his fit chest and arms. This was paired with a nice set of slacks and dress sneakers. He was holding a beautiful potted plant.

"Come on in."

Meow, Yersi added.

Yersi stood just inside the door, tail swishing. Armand looked down at him and laughed lightly. Before coming in, he bent down, holding his hand out to Yersi.

"What's up, Yersi?" he asked in a friendly way.

Yersi's whiskers twitched as he sniffed Armand. After a beat, Yersi rubbed his cheeks back and forth across his hand, and Armand scratched his chin. As he stood back up, Yersi started rubbing against his leg. The cat approved.

"He's cool," Armand said, looking down at him.

Yersi let out another throaty *meow* and trotted into the kitchen.

I laughed and said, "Come on in."

I stepped back to let Armand by, closing the door behind him. Once inside, Armand leaned in to kiss my cheek and gave me a half-hug around the plant. There was a faint, pleasant smell of aftershave, one I knew I was soon going to become addicted to.

"Thanks for having me," he said softly.

"Thanks for coming."

"Here, this is for you." He handed me the plant. "It's lemon beebalm. Laila said you loved to garden. It attracts bees and butterflies and is native to the area."

Unable to help myself, I leaned over and kissed him deeply on the lips.

"Thank you," I said, slightly breathless. This was the first time a date had brought something besides cut flowers or a bottle of wine. It was a truly thoughtful host gift. "It's lovely. I know the perfect spot. Would you like to see the garden?"

Even though it was still warm and slightly humid outside, I figured a plant biologist would probably like to geek out in the garden before the sun set.

"Absolutely," he said just as Yersi also meowed his agreement from the other room.

We both laughed.

I set the plant just outside the backdoor and led Armand through the yard. His eyes lit up as soon as he took in the entire space.

"Wow, Josie!" he exclaimed. "Laila said you had a green thumb, but I never imagined this!"

I blushed slightly at the compliment.

We wove through the garden, talking about plants and pollinators. His hands brushed over the lavender, purposefully crushing the leaves slightly. The smell filled the air.

"I enjoy that smell," he sighed.

"Me, too. My favorite is jasmine. That and the citrus blossoms."

He nodded. "My favorite is peonies. I have several in my yard. My neighbor is taking care of them for me. I hope they survive."

I empathized with him. It was hard leaving my garden to someone else when I traveled. Yersi and the chickens were easy to take care of, but the garden was a fussy thing that needed regular care by someone who had a sixth sense of what the plants needed.

After our short turn around the garden, we headed back inside.

"What can I get you to drink?" I asked as he followed me into the kitchen.

"Water is fine. Thank you."

I poured two glasses and handed him one.

"It smells delicious," he said.

"That's the carnitas. I made Mexican. Hope that's okay?"

"Yes, Mexican is great. Thanks again for cooking. Even though the place I'm renting is fully furnished, it's hard cooking in a kitchen that isn't mine. That's one downside to travel. I like eating from home, and it's tough on the road."

"Do you like to cook?" I asked, curious. I put everything into serving dishes, and he helped me carry them to the table.

"Yes, very much. I like cooking on the grill. I also have a really good cabbage roll recipe. I live off those over the winter. I'm not so good at desserts, though." He shrugged.

"I've never had cabbage rolls. What are those?"

He explained as we sat down and served ourselves. To my delight, everything had turned out perfect. Armand even went for seconds despite the promise of lime bars to follow.

Going into tonight, I'd been a little bit nervous about how the date would go. I didn't often invite people to my home, often preferring the clean cut at the end of a meal out in town. But there was something about Armand that made me immediately comfortable. And, sure enough, we had a wonderful night.

We talked late into the evening. After the meal and dessert, he helped with the dishes, and then we relaxed in the living room. To my immense surprise, Yersi even crawled into his lap and fell asleep. I never once felt like I needed the TV to fill the gaps in conversation or wished he would go. It was actually the opposite. I felt myself hoping that he would stay the night.

We'd been chatting for hours before he finally yawned.

"I'm sorry," he said, looking chagrined. "I'm enjoying our time, but I'm an early bird. It's hard for me to stay up this late."

"Please don't be sorry! I'm also tired. The days of partying late into the night are long over for me." I pulled my phone out to check the time and raised my eyebrows. It was almost midnight. "Holy cow. I had no idea how late it was."

He gently moved Yersi onto the couch next to him, and we both stood. There was a brief awkward pause as we looked at each other. He smiled shyly.

"Thank you again for a lovely evening. I'd love to see you again." He moved closer and clasped one of my hands.

"Thank you for coming," I said, slightly breathless. The touch of his hand on mine was distracting.

He leaned in and pressed his soft lips against mine. What started as a single kiss soon turned into several long ones. I pulled him gently toward me, and he wrapped his arms around my waist.

He leaned back, looking at my face, grazing his fingers down my neck and brushing my hair back slightly.

"I love being here with you," he said, voice catching.

I ran my hand up to the back of his neck and folded him in for another kiss.

"Would you like to stay the night?" I asked, a smile playing across my lips.

"Yes, very much so."

Hands loosely clasped together, I led him back to my room, where the idea of being tired was swept away, and we stayed up well past midnight.

* * *

The next morning, I woke with Armand's gentle breath tickling the hair across the back of my neck and his arms folded around me. I closed my eyes in contentment and snuggled further under the covers. It felt so wonderfully warm and safe.

Yersi was having none of that.

As soon as he heard me wake up, he jumped on the bed, tip-toeing back and forth across us. When that didn't work, he sauntered over to the door and started meowing.

I fumbled for the spray bottle on the bedside table and shot a stream of water at him. If a cat could laugh, he would have; he'd learned how far he could stand and not get spritzed. The meowing intensified.

As I tried to slide out of bed, Armand gently hugged me close and kissed my back before letting me go. I got out of bed and leaned over to kiss his cheek.

"Sorry about Yersi," I whispered.

"It's fine." He smiled softly and reached up to brush my hair back, tracing my ear. "Ileana is worse. She whines to go outside. If I don't get up fast enough, she pees in the house."

I kissed his cheek again and threw on a baggie t-shirt and undies. Sensing victory, Yersi let out a loud *meow* that sounded a lot like the cat version of a "Yes!" and scampered into the kitchen. I shuffled behind him, dug through the fridge, and plopped wet food into his bowl.

Armand was close behind, having thrown on his pants and shirt before joining me. He came up behind me, brushed my hair to the side, and kissed the back of my neck, sending a shiver down my spine. I leaned back into his arms.

"Good morning," I murmured.

"Good morning."

"Would you like some coffee or tea?" I offered.

"Sure, black tea would be perfect if you have it."

I bustled around the kitchen to heat some water and measured out the tea leaves into the strainer. Once the kettle clicked off, I poured the water into the strainer, releasing the sharp smell of the leaves.

"What would you like for breakfast?" I asked, peeking in the fridge as the tea steeped.

"This might be a bit presumptuous…. If you don't mind someone else in your kitchen, I'd like to cook for you."

Surprised at the offer, it took me a moment to respond. "Your wish is my command." I grinned and swept my arm out to the stove.

He grinned back and clamped his hands together. "Excellent!"

Between sips of tea, he whipped us up some omelets with mushrooms, spinach, and feta. I perched in a chair at the counter, guiding him through my kitchen. It wasn't long before he laid out two perfect dishes and joined me. Breakfast was delicious, and we both made quick work of the meal.

"What are you up to today?" he asked casually.

"I have standing plans with my aunty on Sundays. I'll have to leave in about an hour or so. How about you?"

"I was thinking about going for a walk through the Botanic Garden on campus. I was wondering if you wanted to go with me. But family time is important. Raincheck?"

My heart tugged. Though Armand and I had known each other for less than a week, I just couldn't get enough of him. And it sounded like he felt the same way.

"Definitely raincheck. Maybe we can hang out later this week?" I offered hopefully.

"Sounds good. Let me know when you're free, and I'll be there." He smiled and kissed my cheek softly.

I pulled into Aunty's driveway about three hours later, unable to shake the giddy feeling. I knew I'd have a goofy grin on my face for at least a day or two.

Aunty welcomed me at the door with a huge hug as Chula sniffed around my feet.

"You look happy. How are things?" she asked as I followed her inside.

Smiling, heat rose in my cheeks.

"Ohhh," she said softly, eyeing me closely. She arched her eyebrow with a knowing smile. "What's their name?"

She pulled a chair out for me at the table before going around the counter into the kitchen. Potatoes were sizzling in a large pan. In the other, she cracked eggs to fry.

"His name is Armand. He's a plant biologist visiting on a sabbatical. Laila introduced us."

"And?" she asked, bringing me a warm cup of tea before going back to flip the potatoes.

"And…he's pretty amazing. He's wicked smart, he likes gardening, he likes cooking, and, get this, Yersi likes him." I raised an eyebrow.

She turned to look at me, eyes wide, and planted a fist on her hip. "Really?"

"Yup. Even sat on his lap."

She whistled in disbelief.

Yersi was not only a self-described emperor; he was also picky as shit when it came to anyone I might be dating. When I'd brought someone home in the past, he'd just sit on a chair in whatever room we were in and scowl the entire time.

"I'm just glad he makes you happy. You've had a string of shitasses like…." She waved her hand. "What's his name from a week ago?"

My eyebrows creased. "Wyatt?" I was surprised that it took me a beat to recall his name. I'd flushed it along with all of the other failures.

She nodded. "Yeah, him. He's sounded like he just wanted a fuck-me-doll that sat there and said nothing."

"Aunty!" I chided.

"You know I'm right," she said with a self-satisfied grin.

Yeah, I knew she was right. I flashed her a smirk to show she'd won. Dating in my thirties had been rough, and I'd been scraping the bottom of the barrel.

"Armand is different. I keep waiting for the other shoe to drop, but it hasn't yet." I paused, slowly moving my teacup in circles on the table. "I guess him leaving in a few months might be the other shoe."

"Don't miss enjoying the moment because you are fearing the future. Deep breaths. Little steps. Eyes on the prize." She looked at me softly.

She knew me so well and always said just the right thing. I took a sip of the tea, letting the strong scent of mint wash over me.

"So," she continued, "tell me all about him."

I told the story of how we met, our first lunch date, and then dinner last night. About halfway through the tale, she set a large plate of bacon, potatoes, and fried eggs in front of me. Even though I'd eaten just a couple of hours ago, I was starving; I'd burned a lot of calories last night.

"He sounds pretty wonderful. When do I get to meet him?" she asked.

"Aunty, I've only known him for about three seconds."

She picked up her teacup with two hands to take a sip and threw me a knowing look over the rim.

"We'll see." I flashed her a smile and dug into the meal.

I felt the pleasant comfort of the last two days settle over me as I enjoyed idle conversation and a great meal with my favorite person. Chula curled up on my feet, and I couldn't help but sneak her a couple of the potatoes. With our bellies full, we settled back in our chairs, talking books and sipping our drinks. The heat was starting to settle in, and we'd switched to iced tea.

"How's work?" she asked. "Last time you were here, you had a cloud over you."

My stomach sank as the feeling of bliss was gently brushed away with just a few words.

Aunty must have seen my face because she quickly said, "Sorry about that. Didn't mean to bring in bad spirits." She swished her hand in the air as if to brush them away.

"It's all right." I shrugged, knowing she was only trying to look out for me. "The case I was talking to you about last week—I haven't closed it out yet. I'm just hoping we get some answers next week."

"Have any more died?"

"They had one more die on Monday but none since then." I fidgeted with my teacup.

"That's good, then. Whatever it was, it has probably run its course."

I wrinkled my brows and chewed the inside of my cheek. "I hope so. The waiting is the hardest part. I just won't know until we see it through. I'm just hoping I don't come into any more distressed voicemails next week."

I felt the ball of dread pop back up from where it had been hiding. Aunty reached over and grabbed my hand. She caught my eyes, confidence radiating from her.

"You got this." She gave my hand another squeeze.

CHAPTER
NINETEEN

When I rolled into work Monday morning, I was bright-eyed and bushy-tailed after a great weekend with family and friends.

I practically bounced into Dustin's office. Finding it empty, I peeked out on the necropsy floor, leaning over the footbath. Dustin was operating the hoist to lay a horse on the hydraulic table.

"Morning," I called out over the music.

Dustin nodded in greeting, let go of the hoist control, and turned the music down before coming over.

"Mornin', Doc."

"What's that?" I asked cautiously, gesturing toward the horse.

"Racehorse."

I glanced back at the horse and could see the lower rear leg was bent at an odd angle; it was likely a metatarsal fracture.

"Anything else come in?" I asked, anxiety threatening to cloud my good mood.

He shook his head. "Nope."

I was thanking my lucky stars that the horse wasn't from JW Ranch. But then I immediately felt a flash of guilt for being thankful; there was still a dead horse, after all. I couldn't help but feel relief that this death wasn't on me.

As if reading my thoughts, Dustin said, "Thinking about that neuro horse?"

"Yeah," I answered, chewing my inner cheek. "Glad it's an easy case for Dr. Smith. Nothing worse than coming back from vacation with a cooler full of animals."

After running the shop for two weeks, I was glad to be turning it over to Zoe now that she was back from her time off. It'd been a rough go, and I needed a breather.

"Have a nice weekend?" Dustin asked, making casual conversation.

"Pretty good. I had brunch with Aunty. I also went on a date with someone I met through Laila. We had a really nice time." Heat rose in my cheeks at the memory of Armand, and I changed the subject. "Other than that, it was pretty chill. How about you?"

"Went fishing. I caught a nice-sized bass."

"Did you try those new flies you were telling me about?"

His eyes lit up, and we spent about five minutes talking about the difference between foam bass poppers and wooly buggers. I didn't know squat about fishing, other than the fact that I liked fried catfish, and had no idea what the different types of lures were called. But I knew that Dustin loved to talk about fishing, and I liked Dustin.

Just as we were finishing up, Zoe walked up behind me.

"Good morning, Dr. Harjo," she said cheerfully.

"Morning! Good to see you, Dr. Smith." I stepped back and held the door for her as she stepped through the footbath in her coveralls and rubber boots.

"How was vacation?" Dustin asked.

"Fabulous," she said wistfully.

"You look happy and relaxed," I chimed in, smiling. "The pics look amazing."

She beamed. "It *was* pretty amazing."

"Fill me in at lunch? I'm sure you wanna get this knocked out." I pointed to the horse.

"Definitely," Zoe said.

She and Dustin continued chatting as I let the necropsy door close behind me. Back in my office, I dropped into my chair with a sigh of relief. I was off duty this week, and there were no voicemails. I felt a weight lift from my shoulders.

* * *

The morning sped by in an uneventful blur. Grabbing my lunch, I headed to the breakroom. Zoe waved me over to where she was already seated at a table with Dustin and Anna. After zapping my leftover Mexican in the microwave, I joined them.

"That smells delicious," Anna said, moving her lunch over to make space for me.

"Carnitas," I said, holding the container up. Turning to Zoe, I asked, "How was Portland?"

"Fantastic! We drove up through Colorado, Idaho, and Utah on the way there. On the way back, we drove down the coast and then cut over through LA, Arizona, and New Mexico."

"I can't believe you did all of that in two weeks." Anna shook her head.

"Jayden and I took turns, and we had a ton of audiobooks. It was kinda fun, actually—reminded me of the trips I'd go on with my parents."

We all oohed and aahed over pictures on her phone as she told stories from the road. After sharing a chuckle over some misadventures, Zoe asked, "How were things here the last two weeks?"

"Not too bad," I answered.

"It's been pretty slow," Dustin agreed.

"Even with the cops calling?" Zoe asked innocently.

"Who told you the cops called?" I asked, incredulous.

Zoe looked at me with a smirk. "Seriously? Nothing happens in this lab without everyone else knowing."

I snorted a laugh. She had a point.

"The police are investigating an assault charge that may or may not be related to a case I had about a week and a half ago."

"Sooo…." She turned her hand in circles to keep the story going. "Spill it."

"It's a weird one. Sudden death. Four out of sixteen horses," I answered around a bite of carnitas. I went on to explain the findings, or lack, thereof, on necropsy and negative viral testing. I then shared what happened during the visit to the ranch.

"Geez," Zoe said with concern. "I haven't seen a mortality rate like that in horses before. You don't think someone used bait to kill them, do you?"

I fiddled with one of my earrings and hesitated before answering. "I'm not sure. It doesn't feel right. I don't know how to explain it."

"Trust your gut, Doc," Dustin chimed in.

Zoe pointed to him. "What he said."

I huffed a laugh. "Yeah, and just hope we keep up the no-more-deaths streak we've been riding since last Monday."

"Keep me posted?" Zoe asked. "This is an interesting case."

"Definitely," I answered. We were all uber-nerds. Sharing cool lesions was our thing.

With that, the conversation drifted to other things as we finished our meal, and I felt relief to have the spotlight pointing somewhere else.

* * *

After lunch, I put some good tunes on to clear my head and walked to the histology lab to tackle the brain and spinal cord from the Shadowhawk case. I grabbed a lab coat before heading in and snapped some gloves on. One of the techs, Vic, was busy at the embedding station, and we exchanged waves.

Once settled in the fume hood, I peeled back the plastic lids on both buckets.

The brain was resting on the bottom and had a tan tinge. The spinal cord was floating in loose, off-white loops. I fished the brain out and gently peeked into the incision that I had made last week.

Finally!

I let out an audible sigh of relief. It wasn't fixed enough for a neurology study, but it'd do for a diagnostic case. Sometimes, exceptions had to be made for the good of the herd.

I started with the spinal cord, laying each section on paper towels so that I could keep everything in head-to-tail order. Using a histology scalpel, I took several sections of the cervical, thoracic, and lumbar cord, laying them out.

On the upside, the cord looked fully fixed, with no pink tissue. However, everything also looked completely normal. If the cause of death was something like yellow star thistle, I would expect there to be a lesion that I could pick up at trimming, even if very subtle.

I tried to push back a wave of disappointment.

It was still possible that damage to the cord was present, but I'd only be able to see it under the microscope. So, I placed representative sections in cassettes for processing. I rolled the rest of the cord up in the paper towels and dropped the segments back into the formalin.

I wiped the cutting board off and moved on to the brain. Crossing my fingers, I grabbed a bread knife and made even serial sections from front to back. I laid the sections out on the cutting board in order and examined them closely.

The outer edges of the brain were a nice gray color from fixation. The innermost parts were still slightly pink despite sitting in formalin for over a week. I decided to push them through anyway; I might get the slides back tomorrow if I was lucky.

I examined the sections carefully. On the left side of one of the frontal lobe sections, there was a small area of brownish discoloration, and the tissue of the white matter looked collapsed. Another small focus of discoloration marred the white matter of the parietal lobe.

Holy shit.

I was pretty sure I'd finally found a lesion: leukoencephalomalacia, which was a snooty way of saying "soft, white matter of the brain." Not a lot of things would cause a lesion like this. I felt an adrenaline dump, and my heart rate sped up. I was pretty sure I knew what had killed these horses, but I'd need to look at the brain under the microscope to be certain.

I carefully collected sections of affected and unaffected areas of the brain. I dropped the sections in a rack to fix until the night run on the processor and flagged them as STAT.

After cleaning up my station, I tracked down one of the histology techs. Since the other two techs started early, Vic was the only one still around.

"Hey, Vic."

He stopped cutting the block on the microtome and turned to me with a smile. "Hello, Dr. Harjo. What's up?"

"I just put sections of brain and spinal cord from a horse in the fixing ring. Any chance we can try to get them on the processor tonight? They're urgent."

"How fixed are they?" he asked. He knew me too well.

Slightly chagrined, I said, "Enough...? Hopefully?"

"I'll check them before I put them on but will do my best to push them through," he answered.

"Thanks, Vic. Appreciate it."

We knuckle-bumped with our gloves. As much as I wanted to rush things, we needed to wait until the sections were fixed enough, and I trusted Vic to make that call. If we pushed the sections through too soon, the slides might be a total loss, and I'd have to trim new sections in, delaying things further.

* * *

As I headed out of the histology lab, I almost ran headlong into Zoe.

"Hey," Zoe said, surprised.

I stopped to chat. "Hey, Zoe. Just trimmed that horse brain in."

"Ohhh! And?" Her eyes lit up with curiosity.

"There were some subtle lesions in the white matter of the brain. I'm pretty sure it's leukoencephalomalacia. I'm hoping histo will come back tomorrow to confirm."

"That's wild," she said, shaking her head slightly.

"I know," I agreed. "I'm just glad I found *something*. It's been a frustrating week or so."

Gerald slithered out of nowhere, pushing his way into our conversation. I had no idea what the guy did all day long. He always seemed poised to pounce anytime a woman was in the hallway.

"Hello, Dr. Smith." He nodded to Zoe before turning to me. "Dr. Harjo." His eyes slithered up and down my blouse and jeans.

"Is there something that you need, Gerald?" I huffed.

"Oh, yes." The slimy grin dropped from his face. "I just happened to overhear that you finally found something in the neuro horse."

"Looks like leukoencephalomalacia," I said tersely. "I'm waiting on histo to confirm."

"You better be pretty sure now that the police are involved," he counseled. "There are plenty of things that can cause that many horses to die."

Zoe crossed her arms and said, "Yeah? Like what?"

"Plenty of things." He threw her a dismissive look. "I'm just saying that this is an important case."

"Yes, Gerald. I'm very much aware of that," I interrupted.

I was losing my temper. I'd finally started to shed the shroud of stress and anxiety around this case, and Gerald was fighting to keep it hanging around my shoulders.

"I just want to make sure that you've considered all of the possible differentials," he said from his high horse.

"She has, Gerald. Stick to your lane," Zoe warned.

He crossed his arms and huffed. "Well, if you need any help, you know where my office is."

Zoe snorted.

I flashed her a warning look; poking the bear never ended well.

Sure enough, Gerald's body posture changed, and a leer stretched across his face. "By the way, that is a lovely outfit, Dr. Harjo."

I pressed my lips together, looking for an escape.

"You sure know how to dress yourself in a flattering way," he continued. "That outfit accentuates your body. You must turn heads wherever you go."

"Not appropriate, Dr. Richter," Zoe said, her voice suddenly icy cold.

"Now, now. Don't be jealous. Dr. Harjo has a perfect body." He swept his hand up and down in my direction. "One that could never be replicated with artificial hormones." He shot a pointed glance at Zoe.

Zoe bristled.

Sensing a fight about to erupt, I stepped in between them. "Enough," I hissed.

I clasped Zoe's hand, trying to catch her eye, and pulled her into my office. Closing the door behind me, I asked, "Are you okay?"

Tears welled up in her eyes. "I can't help the body I was born in."

I pulled her into a hug. She slumped into a chair, and I passed her some Kleenex.

"People say nasty things all the time. You'd think I'd be used to it." She shook her head and wiped her eyes.

"Doesn't make it right. Also doesn't mean it doesn't hurt."

She drew a deep breath. "Rise above it," she said to herself. She threw her shoulders back and flipped her hair. "He's a sad little man. And I have lots of people around me who love me. Fuck it."

"Yeah, fuck it." I grinned and squeezed her hand. "You are beautiful, and you are loved."

"Thanks, Josie." She folded me into another hug.

After making sure Zoe was in a good place, we parted ways, and I went to confront the dragon. I tolerated his shit when I was the target, but no way in hell was I going to let him treat Zoe that way.

I knocked on Gerald's closed door. After he called out, "Enter," I went in and shut the door behind me. I'd taken deep breaths to chase away the bulk of my rage, but I still had a low level of anger burning through me. It took everything in me not to slam the door.

"Dr. Harjo," Gerald said. Surprise flashed across his face, which was quickly replaced by a smug look. "Come for advice on the neuro case?" He leaned back in his chair, folding his hands at the back of his neck.

"Nope," I said brusquely. "I wanted to talk about what happened with Zoe."

He dropped his arms to the armrests, his eyes narrowing.

I pressed on. "It's not appropriate to talk about the way she looks or make inappropriate comments about her gender. It's hurtful."

"So?" he said defensively and crossed his arms.

"Look, man. Cut that shit out, or I'm going to report you. It'll start with Fran, and if she keeps doing nothing, I'll take it as high as it needs to go. This crap stops now," I said, tapping my pointer finger on his desk. "Leave Zoe alone." I felt the adrenaline surge again.

He met me with silence. We stared each other down for a beat. It took everything in my power not to cross my arms and hunch my shoulders under his glare.

He looked away first, and I gestured to his computer. "I'll leave you to it."

* * *

Today had been a rollercoaster of emotions, and I practically crawled out of my car and into my home. Yersi, sensing my distress, made a beeline for the kitchen without a single peep. Trying to reward the good behavior, I fed him before I kicked my shoes off and collapsed on the couch.

I sat there, staring at the ceiling for who knows how long, when the ringing of my phone startled me into action. It was Armand. Today had been a rough go, and I wasn't sure I wanted to unload on him.

Screw it.

"Hey," I answered, hearing the smile in my voice regardless of the crappy day I was having.

"Hey," he answered softly, making my heart lurch. "I miss you."

"Miss you, too." I felt myself recenter at the sound of his voice.

"How are you?" he asked with a slight tinge of worry. "You sound tired."

"Today was rough," I conceded.

"Was it that case?"

"Actually, I'm pretty sure I have that one in the bag," I answered, a bit of joy springing back up. "It's just office politics."

"Want to talk about it?" he asked.

"Not really, sorry. I need to go through detox first."

"Ouch. That bad?" he asked, sympathy filling his voice.

"Yeah. That bad," I said, unable to hide the downward inflection in my voice.

"I'm here if you need me," he offered.

"Thank you." My heart warmed, and my shoulders relaxed. It felt good to know I wasn't alone. "Want to catch up later this week?"

"Very much so. Are you free Wednesday for dinner?" he asked.

Wednesday is so far away! I thought, realizing how drunk I was with this guy. *But he's drunk, too.* I smiled to myself, grateful for the distraction.

"Sure. If you're sick of eating out, want me to cook again? I'm off duty this week. It'll be no sweat."

"That sounds great. Thanks. I remember you saying you liked games. Want to play one when I come over?"

I felt my cheeks warm as my mind went where it shouldn't.

"I didn't bring any games with me," he said, filling the silence. "But I can buy one. Is there one you want to play but haven't tried yet?"

I felt myself relaxing into the conversation. It was pretty cool that he remembered that I liked games. "Up to you. What kind of games do you like?"

"I'll play almost anything…. Well…not Monopoly." He laughed. "I like strategy games. I'm pretty good at chess, too."

"I've got tons of those. How about you come over, and we can pick one of mine?" I offered.

"Perfect. I can't wait to see you again. Hope the rest of your day gets better."

It already has.

CHAPTER
TWENTY

Tuesday morning, I went straight to the histology lab, hoping the Shadowhawk slides were ready. Two of the histology technicians started bright and early. If the cassettes had made it into the processor last night, there was a very slim chance that they might already be finished.

When I walked in the door, Sally was cutting blocks. Noah was pulling racks out of the stainer and setting them out to dry.

"Morning, Noah. Any chance the brain and spinal cord I trimmed in yesterday made it on the run last night?" I asked.

"Good morning, Dr. Harjo. Yes, ma'am." He nodded to the rack that was slowly dipping through the various stain solutions in the auto-stainer. "They're staining now and should come off soon. Want me to bring them to you when they're finished?"

"Yes, please. Thanks!" I flashed him a grateful smile and returned to my office.

I tried to keep myself busy and work on my endocrine lectures for the fall, but I was practically bouncing in my seat, waiting for the slides. About thirty minutes later, Noah saved me from myself and dropped the flats on my desk.

"Careful. The glue might be a little wet," he said.

Usually, the slides were left to air-dry to let the coverslip glue set before they were stacked into flats. He'd done me a solid by bringing them to me so quickly. I'd have to be careful that the wet glue didn't get on my microscope lenses.

"Thanks, Noah. Appreciate it."

"Anytime," he said as he closed the door behind him.

I flipped open both flats, looking for the sections of the brain that had the gross lesions. Picking one up, the glue stuck to my fingers slightly as I placed it on the microscope stage.

I let out a loud sigh of relief.

There was extensive liquefactive necrosis of the white matter in the affected sections of the brain. The necrotic areas were surrounded by rims of hemorrhage, and there was minimal inflammation. The histologic changes were classic for leukoencephalomalacia. All these fancy words added up to one thing: my suspicions were correct.

There was one thing that caused a lesion like that in horse brains, and it was fumonisin toxicity. Sandy had been right about those swollen feed pellets. They'd somehow gotten wet and were growing mold, making the fumonisin toxin. I'd bet dollars to donuts that the fumonisin concentrations on the feed came back in the toxic range.

I scanned through the rest of the slides just to make sure I wasn't missing anything, like an infection or cancer. There was no evidence of inflammation to suggest viral infection, which I had pretty much ruled out already. The spinal cord was relatively uneventful.

I leaned back in my chair, feeling my shoulders relax. It hadn't been the ranch hand or the owners after all; it was a very unfortunate case of moldy feed. Now, all I had to do was get that fumonisin test back on the pelleted feed to confirm the source, and I'd be golden. One last little piece needed to fall into place, and I could put this case to bed.

Eager to share the news, I looked up the number for JW Ranch and dialed it. After five rings, I was sent to voicemail. I left a quick message.

"Hello, Mr. Williams. This is Dr. Harjo from the diagnostic lab. I just wanted to give you a heads-up that I'm fairly certain that Shadowhawk died from eating moldy feed. It could explain the deaths of the other horses, too. So, please make sure that you don't feed any more of the pelleted feed. Save any bags of feed you have and write down the lot numbers. Call me back when you get this. I'll be in the office until around five today and then back early tomorrow."

I left the number for the lab, hung up, and then picked the phone right back up to call Charlie.

"Willow Park Mobile. How can I help you?" the receptionist answered.

"Hello. This is Dr. Harjo from the diagnostic lab. Is Dr. Anderson in?"

"No, ma'am. Would you like to call his cell or leave a message?"

"I have his cell number. I'll give him a jingle."

I sifted through the sticky notes on my desk, looking for Charlie's cell number. The adrenaline surge had faded, and now my hands were shaky. I kicked myself for not putting Charlie's number in my private phone.

Clasping the purple sticky note in hand, I dialed Charlie's cell.

"Doc Anderson here."

"Hey, Charlie. It's Josie."

"Hello, Dr. Harjo. How can I help you?"

"I'm pretty sure I know what's going on at JW Ranch. I just got the histo back on the brain and spinal cord, and there's leukoencephalomalacia."

"Hot damn," Charlie said in disbelief.

"Yep," I replied. "I am pretty sure it's fumonisin toxicity. We already sent the pelleted feed out for testing and should have confirmation sometime this week."

"Did you talk to Mr. Williams yet? How'd he take it?"

"I just left a message. It's critical that he saves any feed bags he's got. The lab report should help any claim he files with the feed company. But he's gotta have the lot numbers and stuff."

"Yes, ma'am. I'll give him a call in a bit, too." He huffed a low laugh of relief. "Between you and me, the owners were actin' so squirrely that I kinda thought it might've been malicious."

"Honestly, I was worried about that, too, especially after Sandy found that bait. I guess the ranch hand is off the hook?"

"For Shadowhawk, at least," he mused. "The kicker is going to be proving the death of the other three horses that Mr. Williams buried. And the ranch hand still has those assault charges hanging over him."

I hummed in agreement. "The insurance and feed companies will likely have to duke it out. Anyway, if you call Mr. Williams, please remind him to not use the pelleted feed and save any bags."

"Yes, ma'am. This was a tough case. Thanks for the help, Josie." I could hear the relief and sincerity in his voice. Despite having seen just about everything in his career, this case had been wearing on him, too.

"Anytime," I said with a tad of pride. "I'll call you when I get the fumonisin results back."

As soon as the phone hit the cradle, I was out of my seat and heading down to Sandy's office to poke my head in. Unable to find her at her desk or in the toxicology lab, I left her a quick note explaining the findings on histology.

It wasn't until Wednesday that everything finally came together.

CHAPTER
TWENTY-ONE

A red light winked ominously from my desk phone Wednesday morning. I couldn't help but feel a surge of concern. Even though I was pretty certain I knew what was killing the horses at the JW Ranch, I'd be anxious until I had the fumonisin results from the feed in hand.

I shucked off my purse and slumped into my chair. With a sliver of dread, I put in the passcode to listen to the voicemail.

"Dr. Harjo. This is Adam from JW Ranch. I got your message about the feed. I don't have any of the bags left. The feed company came by and picked them up right after y'all left last week. They paid us for them, and since you said we shouldn't feed it anymore, we didn't think it was a big deal. Call me back and let us know what we should do."

He left his number and hung up without saying goodbye. I slowly placed the phone in the cradle in slight shock. I practically face-palmed my forehead as I realized the truck we saw when leaving the ranch was probably from the feed company.

Those fuckers. The feed company *knew* and was trying to cover it up by buying back all the bags and not issuing a recall.

That's why the bags looked fine, I realized. The pellets had probably gotten wet in the warehouse before the bags were filled. And, if the feed company already knew before JW Ranch said anything, that meant other animals had probably gotten sick or even died. I was now more certain than ever that the fumonisin concentrations in the feed would be in the toxic range.

I picked the phone back up and dialed Adam's number. After a few rings, I got his voicemail. I guessed we'd be playing phone tag.

"Hello, Mr. Williams. This is Dr. Harjo from the diagnostic lab. I received your message. The testing on the feed is still pending. But, given that the feed company took all of your remaining bags, that only increases the index of suspicion. Please let me know if they said anything about why they were taking the bags back. I know the brand is Best in Class. But, if you have any more information about it, please call me back." I left my number, even though he probably had it memorized now, and added a goodbye.

As soon as I hung up the phone, I heard a confident knock at the door.

"Come in," I called out.

Sandy poked her head in. "Got a minute?"

"Yeah, sure. What's up?" I gestured to the other chair, and she sat.

"The fumonisin results are back on the neuro horse," she said. Her posture was relaxed, but there was a definite gleam in her eye. "The concentration was extremely high, confirming fumonisin toxicity."

"Hot shit, Sandy!" The final puzzle piece landed in place with a *thud.*

"I just checked again, and the feed company still hasn't issued a recall. Any chance the owner can get us the lot numbers off those bags?" she asked.

"The bags are all gone." I shook my head and then added, "The company must've known about it for a while."

"Huh? How so?" she asked.

I shook my head again, unable to hide my anger. "I just got a call from the owner. The feed company picked up all the bags the same day we were there. Remember that truck pulling in when we were leaving?"

She nodded.

"That was them picking it all up. I'm sure they've known for a week or more!" I couldn't keep the frustration from my voice. "A rep also called me last week, asking about the case. What was his name…." I shifted through the sticky notes on my desk. "Something Jones…I wrote his number down." Unable to find the note in question, I shook my head, frustrated. "I must have thrown it away. Damn."

Sandy just looked sad. "Unfortunately, I'm not surprised that the feed company knew about it and just bought it all back from JW Ranch. That's the M.O. for the shadier companies. I've even seen them come out to feedlots with vacuums to get every last bit." She pursed her lips in thought. "You know…I vaguely remember the owner bringing the feed sample still in the original bag. Do you remember?"

I slapped my hand lightly on my desk. "Yes! They did! Any chance you still have it?"

"Maybe…. If I remember right, it was a pretty big bag. I'll go check."

"Thanks for everything, Sandy."

"Teamwork makes the dream work." She flashed me a smile before heading out.

Just after lunch, there was another knock on my door. Sandy poked her head in once again.

"Coming to the faculty meeting?" she asked.

"Oh! Yes! Thanks for grabbing me. Just a tad distracted today." I gathered my iPad and stylus before following her out. "Any luck with finding the feed bag?"

A huge grin spread across her face. "Actually…yes. The techs had emptied the feed into an air-tight container, but Eva cut the label out and put it in with the feed before tossing the rest of the bag. We've got the lot number."

"Absolutely fantastic," I said.

Sandy nodded. "And…I called the feed company just before coming to grab you. They were super cagey and wouldn't share anything with me. But...." She gave me a mischievous look. "I also called my buddy at the FDA. Turns out, the company hasn't issued any recalls yet. I sent over the results, and the FDA will be issuing a warning by end-of-day."

"Damn, Dr. Bishop! You go!"

"Shame on them," she said, unable to keep the anger from her voice. "They should've acted earlier. They had to have known, coming to pick up what was left a week ago."

"Covering their tracks," I huffed, shaking my head.

"They'll get theirs," she said. "Let's hustle to the meeting. You've got a victory lap to run, and you don't want to be late."

* * *

When we all settled down for the meeting, we had a full house. All of the lab section heads, pathologists, and Fran settled around the table, with Zoe sitting as far from Gerald as possible. Fran began with the usual announcements and roundtable updates from the lab section heads.

With the routine stuff out of the way, Fran went straight for me. "Any updates on the neuro horse, Josie?"

"Actually, yes," I said, trying not to sound self-congratulatory.

Zoe and Tom leaned in.

Before I could continue, Gerald jumped in. "It's about time. How many had to die while you were fumbling around trying to figure it out?"

Zoe let out a loud, irritated sigh and threw daggers at Gerald with her eyes.

Gerald crossed his arms and huffed.

Trying to push politics aside, I pressed on. "There was evidence of leukoencephalomalacia on histology. We confirmed toxic concentrations of fumonisin B1 in the pelleted feed."

"Wow!" Tony exclaimed. "I've never seen fumonisin take out so many animals that fast before."

"The concentrations were fairly high—26 ppm," Sandy chimed in.

"I think that's why the horses had little to no clinical signs before death."

"What about the other horses?" Zoe asked, eyebrows creased. "Are they still at risk?"

"I think any horse that ate that feed is at risk," I said, looking at Sandy, who nodded in agreement. "They might've received a lower dose and be in the clear. But Charlie over at Willow Park is going to have to keep an eye on them for a while."

"We may get some stragglers in over the next month or so, then," Zoe mused.

"It's possible," Sandy said. "Josie advised them to stop using that feed on day one. Her quick action reduced the exposure and most assuredly saved lives. We may be through the thick of it."

I felt a flush creep into my cheeks. Sandy didn't hand out compliments too often. After almost two weeks of stress over this case, it felt good to know that I might have made a difference.

"Excellent job, Josie," Fran added.

"And you thought it was the ranch hand or the owner," Gerald tutted. "I could have told you it wasn't intentional."

Sandy shot him a glare this time, and he clamped his mouth shut. There were some boundaries even Gerald wasn't willing to cross; pissing off someone as well-respected as Sandy was one of them.

Trying to diffuse the situation, Tom changed the subject. "The insurance company is going to have a field day with the feed company."

Heads nodded around the table.

"I don't pity the feed company," Sandy said gruffly. "They knew about this well before today."

"Agreed," I added. "The feed company took all the bags from the ranch about a week ago. And the FDA hadn't heard a peep about it until today when Sandy called them."

"Have they issued the recall yet?" Fran asked.

"They said they would have it out by the end of the day," Sandy replied.

"Excellent," Fran said, rapping her knuckles lightly on the table. "Great job, everyone."

* * *

After the faculty meeting, I called Charlie and Adam, leaving messages for both about the fumonisin results and the impending FDA warning. I typed up the final report for the Shadowhawk case, grateful to have all of the pieces fall neatly into place. Hitting release on that magnum opus felt awesome. Now, it was up to the powers that be to make that feed company pay for all the damage they'd done.

I left work a bit early, still floating on cloud nine. The case was in the bag, and I felt all of the weight I'd been carrying since talking to Mr. Williams in the interview room float off my shoulders.

Plus, Armand was coming over for dinner.

I'd had some chicken marinating overnight. I tossed that on the grill while I prepped red beans and rice and a citrus salad with jicama. Yersi lay sprawled out by the backdoor, tail swishing languidly. He knew we were having a guest tonight by all the hustle and bustle. I hoped he'd be happy once he saw who it was.

The doorbell rang at six on the dot, and I felt my stomach flutter. I tried and failed to wipe the goofy grin off my face. Today was just too awesome not to be bouncing with happiness.

Armand stood at the door, smiling. The scent of his aftershave swept over me.

"Hey," I said, suddenly feeling like I was sixteen again.

"Hello," he answered. He leaned in to give me a deep kiss.

Yeah, it didn't get much better than this.

ACKNOWLEDGMENTS

As always, oodles of thanks go to my family. To Derek Smith, thank you for the many hours at Bueno Café, talking through plot lines and character development. Once again, this book wouldn't be what it is without you. To Justin Smith, thank you for your patience as I talked (and fretted) about the book incessantly. Thanks for loving me despite the necropsy knife I keep on my desk. I have to say, with your swords on the wall, the necropsy knife really ties the room together. To Tyler Dryden, I always appreciate your artistic touch. Thank you for helping me with the branding and the merch. And, as always, for being the sunshine that keeps me going when I start doubting myself. I appreciate all of you!

This story may seem heavy-handed with the sexual harassment, sexism, transphobia, and racism in the workplace. I admit, I was a bit nervous writing about those topics. But I felt like this story wouldn't be truthful without those pieces. Every sexist remark and act of sexual harassment by a character in this book has been said or done to me at some point in my career. Further, the acts of racism and transphobia are events I have personally witnessed. I hope that people read this and see the truth. By acknowledging the experience of those in marginalized groups, we can endeavor to make all workplaces more inclusive. This is our opportunity to stand up for ourselves and others.

The character of Dr. Sandy Bishop is inspired by my two favorite toxicologists: Drs. Karyn Bischoff and Sandra Morgan. I hope Sandy Bishop did you both proud! Many thanks to Dr. Karyn Bischoff who ventured from her usual journal article writing/reviewing to make sure that all of the toxicology pieces in this fictitious novel were scientifically accurate. I'll forever remember her email about the first few chapters in which she recommended that I add a very specific differential. Little did she know what awaited her at the end of the story! Just further proof that she is a kickass toxicologist.

Heaps of gratitude go out to my mentors: Drs. Linda Munson and Don Schlafer. When I worked on the pathology floor as an undergraduate, Linda pulled me aside to encourage me to apply to veterinary school. One never knows how a single conversation can change the course of one's life. Her fingerprints are all over my career, and I always hope I can pay that forward. Don took me under his wing during my residency and grew my love for reproductive pathology. His mentorship led to dozens of publications in the field. I also want to thank all of the others who have had a positive impact on my life as a pathologist: Drs. Jim MacLachlan, Brad Njaa, Ana Alcaraz, Bill Johnson, Roger Panciera, Steve Smith, and all of the other brilliant (and kind!) pathologists out there. Thank you for helping me every step of the way.

Thank you to my copy editor, Caryn Pine. I appreciate you taking this foray into a mystery novel with me; I couldn't have done it without your help! Typos are my Achilles heel, and I'm sending heaps of gratitude to Yasmine Bonatch who proofread the book. Her keen attention to detail saved me from that all-to-common public embarrassment. Finally, Gareth Clegg did a fantastic job on the cover design. I know my request to have a legit necropsy knife on the cover might've been a little weird, but he made it work! He also formatted the interior of the book for both the eBook and print formats. He can be found at www.garethclegg.com. Thank you all for polishing everything up.

And to everyone who has read this far through the book, thank you for going on this journey. I hope you find joy in the small things, appreciate differences, and put a little more kindness out into the world. And, if one or two people are inspired to become a veterinary pathologist after reading this, all the better!

ABOUT THE AUTHOR

Catherine Sequeira was born and raised in the Bay Area. She obtained her BS and DVM from UC Davis and completed an anatomic pathology residency at Cornell. Throughout her career, she has lived and worked in Switzerland, New York, Oklahoma, and Scotland before returning to California. With over twenty years as a veterinary anatomic pathologist under her belt, she now writes and teaches. In her spare time, she enjoys reading sci-fi and fantasy, playing tabletop games, and gardening. She lives in Northern California with her partner, son, cat, and dragon (the bearded kind, that is).

She can be found online at
https://www.catherinesequeira.com